Harvard Episodes

Also from Westphalia Press

westphaliapress.org

Harvard Episodes

by Charles Macomb Flandrau

WESTPHALIA PRESS
An imprint of Policy Studies Organization

Harvard Episodes
All Rights Reserved © 2014 by Policy Studies Organization

Westphalia Press
An imprint of Policy Studies Organization
1527 New Hampshire Ave., NW
Washington, D.C. 20036
info@ipsonet.org

ISBN-13: 978-1-63391-065-2
ISBN-10: 1633910652

Cover design by Taillefer Long at Illuminated Stories:
www.illuminatedstories.com

Daniel Gutierrez-Sandoval, Executive Director
PSO and Westphalia Press

Devin Proctor, Director of Media and Publications
PSO and Westphalia Press

Updated material and comments on this edition
can be found at the Westphalia Press website:
www.westphaliapress.org

HARVARD EPISODES

BY

CHARLES MACOMB FLANDRAU

BOSTON
COPELAND AND DAY
MDCCCXCVII

To W. A.

DEAR W. A.   I have written about a very little corner of a very great place; but one that we knew well, and together.

C. M. F.

CONTENTS

Harvard Episodes

THE CHANCE

TWO men were talking in a room in Claverly Hall. Horace Hewitt, the sophomore who owned the apartment, had passed, during the hour with his visitor, from the state in which conversation is merely a sort of listless chaffing to where it becomes eager, earnest, and perplexing. The other, a carefully dressed, somewhat older young man, across whose impassive, intellectual profile a pair of eye-glasses straddled gingerly, was not, perhaps, monopolising more than his share of the discussion, for Robinson Curtiss was the kind of person to whom a large conversational portion was universally conceded; but he was, without doubt, talking with a continuance and an air of authority that unconsciously had become relentless. Both men were smoking: Hewitt, a sallow meerschaum pipe, with

his class in raised letters on the bowl;
Curtiss, a cigarette he had taken from the
metal case he still held meditatively in his
hand. He smoked exceedingly good
cigarettes, and practised the thrifty art of
always discovering just one in his case.

"So you think my college life from an
undergraduate's standpoint, and it's the
only standpoint I give that for," — Hewitt
snapped his fingers impatiently, — "will
always be as much of a fizzle as it has so
far?" He had jumped up from the big
chair in which he had all along been
sprawling and stood before Robinson in
an attitude that was at once incredulous
and despairing. The momentary embarrassment that Curtiss felt at this unexpected show of feeling on the part of his
young friend, took the form of extreme
deliberation in returning his cigarette-case
to his pocket, and in repeating the performance of lighting his cigarette that had
not gone out.

He had not been a graduate quite three
years in all, but that had been ample time
— particularly as it had been spent far
from Cambridge — for the readjustment
of certain views of his, — views in which

four eventful years at college had been grotesquely prominent. He found, on returning to the university town, that his absence rendered him frequently indifferent to the genuineness and importance, not merely of the more delicate problems of the undergraduate world, — it was one of these on which he was at the present moment indiscreetly touching, — but even to the obvious and common incidents of the academic experience: to the outcome of examinations, to the degree of Bachelor of Arts. It was not until Hewitt stood troubled and expectant before him that Curtiss appreciated how tactless the disparity in their knowledge of things collegiate had made him appear to his young friend. A sudden reminiscent intuition, that flashed him back to his own sophomore year, caused him to feel that what he was saying to Hewitt was almost brutal; in his capacity of a young graduate he had indulged in a cold-blooded lecture (it could hardly be called a discussion) on questions that very properly were not questions to a fellow in Hewitt's situation, but warm, operative realities. Hewitt was in many ways such a mature young person, his valuation of other people and their actions had always seemed so temperate, so just, that Curtiss, without knowing it, had simply ignored the fellow's healthy undergraduate attitude. He had failed to assume how eager the sophomore was to be some active part of the new and fascinating life going on everywhere about him; how completely he was possessed by the indefinable, disquieting, stimulative spirit that so triumphantly inhibits Harvard from becoming a mere place of learning. Curtiss had spent the evening in throwing what he sincerely believed was a searching light on some aspects of Harvard life; he was beginning to wish he had allowed Hewitt to perform the office for himself.

"Be honest with me, Curtiss." Hewitt spoke in the distinct, simple tones that as a rule accompany words one hesitates to trifle with. "You 've gone through the whole damn thing yourself, and got more out of it — not more than you deserve, of course, but more than most men get; you knew everybody and belonged to — to —" Hewitt hesitated a moment; any single college institution — social, athletic,

or intellectual — did not in itself forcibly
appeal to him ; there was something petty
in particularising. " You belonged to —
to everything, when you were in college,"
he finally said ; " how was it done — how
is it done every day ? I see it going on
around me all the time; but I can't touch
it in any way, — it never comes near
enough, if you know what I mean ; and
what I can't explain to myself is that
I don't see why it should come any nearer
to me, — only, I want it to." The manner in which Horace blurted out the last
few words was an epitome of the situation ;
their confession of keen longing to know
and be known in his class had gathered in-
tensity with the growing suspicion that certain conditions of the place — conditions
he felt rather than understood — were every
day making the realisation of his desire
for activity, acquaintances, friendship, more
impossible. His great common sense —
in Hewitt the quality amounted to a sort
of prosaic talent — would always preclude
his degenerating into one of the impo-
tently rebellious ; it had kept him free
from the slightest tinge of bitterness
toward any one, but it had not made his

interminable, solitary walks up Brattle
Street (there was apparently no other walk
to take in Cambridge) less interminable;
it had enlivened none of the stolid evenings in his rooms which, with a necessary
amount of study, a chapter or two from
some book he did not much care about,
and a bottle of beer, always came to an end
somehow or other in spite of themselves;
it had not invested stupid theatres with
interest, nor mediocre athletics with excitement.   Common sense, the prevailing
trait of Hewitt's character, that induced
the middle-aged to consider him "singularly well balanced for a young man," was
quite powerless to dispel the desperate
loneliness of his sophomore year.   His
common sense was a coat of mail that defied sabre thrusts, perhaps, but let in the
rain.

"You know everything, Rob," Hewitt
smiled; he had after all no wish to appear
emotional.   "Is there something the matter with me, or with Harvard, that has kept
me what you very well know I am — an
isolated nonentity who has rather begun
to lose hope?   Are there other fellows in
college who are gentlemen, and used to all

the word implies, but who might be in any one of the fifteen leading universities of Kansas, for all the good they are getting out of this place? If I had only been given a chance — " he broke out with sudden vehemence, — " a good, square chance, the kind a man has a right to expect when he enters college — to meet my equals equally — to make myself felt and liked if I had the power to, why I should n't mind failing, you know, not in the least; a man who is n't an ass accepts chronic unpopularity as he does chronic red hair, or any other personal calamity." Hewitt's own locks had sufficient colour to lend authority to his statement. " It is n't that — it 's the utter impossibility, as far as I can see, of a boy who came here as I did, getting a fair trial. Every day I am more and more convinced that my prospects for the broad, enlightening sort of existence I expected to find on entering Harvard were about as definite and as brilliant as the prospects of a stillborn child on entering the world. What 's the matter? What 's wrong? Who 's to blame? "

There was an admirable force to Hewitt's

manner when he was thoroughly in earnest that, as a rule, roused even in Curtiss a vague apprehension that sincerity
was, somehow, obligatory. It did not
restrain him, however, from assuming
an expression of mock helplessness and
murmuring, —

"It 's so long — so intricate."

"If people only knew what they were in
for before they came," Hewitt continued.

"Maybe they would n't come," suggested the other.

"Of course they 'd come, — the place
is too great, — they could n't afford to stay
away." Horace passed over the axioms
with the impatience of one who has problems to solve. "Of course they would
come," he repeated ; "but they would
come with their eyes opened — they
would know what not to expect ; that 's
the important thing."

"Ah, but who could do it ? Who
would do it ? It would be like assisting
a new kitten to see by means of a pin.
We must all work out our own salvations,"
Curtiss added sententiously.

"That brings it right round to my
point again," exclaimed Hewitt.   "Of

course every man wants to 'work out his own salvation,' as you put it; but at Harvard I don't think it's every man who is given the opportunity to. He does n't know that before he comes, he does n't find it out for some time after he gets here; but it's true, and it's precisely what I want you to tell me about — to explain." There was but a faint note of triumph in Hewitt's voice; he realised that he had Curtiss in a corner, but he had not been conscious of manœuvring to get him there. "Tell me this: Do you think that Harvard — and by that I don't mean the Officers of Instruction and Government, they 're the least of it — do you think that Harvard is fair, and do you think that it is American?"

There was something so general, so meaningless, so senatorial in the application of Hewitt's final word that Curtiss was surprised into a shout of laughter.

"Whether it's fair or not, depends on who 's telling you about it," he said gravely enough; "but there 's no question as to its nationality," he laughed again; "of course it 's American, horribly American, deliciously American!"

Hewitt puckered his forehead and waited for more ; he did not in the least understand.

" When I say American, I don't mean what you mean ; because — pardon me for saying it — you don't mean anything." Curtiss found it suddenly easy to rattle on as he had been doing earlier in the evening; his laugh had cleared the atmosphere. " My dear fellow," he said, " Harvard University possesses its labouring class, its middle class, and its aristocracy, as sharply, as inevitably, as — as — " he was about to draw a rather over-emphatic comparison between Harvard and the social orders of Sparta in the days of Lycurgus, when Hewitt, still puzzled, broke in with, —

" But if that's the case, it is n't American at all — you contradict yourself in the same breath."

" I assumed that you knew more about your own country," Curtiss remarked with dry superiority; " I sha'n't undertake to discuss the social system of the United States; it would simply necessitate my going over a lot of platitudes that would bore us both. It's only when we apply to our college, what we all know to be so undeniable of the country at large, that the situation at once becomes novel and preposterous to so many people. The conventional idea of an American college — you know this because the idea was yours before you came here — is that it consists of a multitude of lusty young men linked together by the indissoluble bonds of class and college, all striving, shoulder to shoulder, for the same ends, in a general way,— just what the ends are I don't think the public cares very much, but they 're presumably charmingly unpractical and fine,— and living in an intoxicating atmosphere of intimacy, a robust sense of loyalty that is supposed to pervade the academic groves and render them the temporary home of a great, lighthearted, impulsive, congenial brotherhood. Well, I don't know whether other American institutions of learning answer the description, because I 've never been to them; but Harvard does n't, n t in the slightest particular."

"Then I wish it would n't attempt to," murmured Hewitt.

"There is no attempt," answered Curtiss ; " there is merely a pretence,— a pretence that, strangely enough, is n't meant to deceive any one. We find it in the naïve untruthfulness of the college papers, in the eloquent conventionality of the Class Day Orators ; the college press prattles about 'class feeling' and all the other feelings that none of us, since the place has grown so large, has ever felt ; the orator's sentiments bear about the same relation to real life that his gestures do : he has a lot to say about everybody's sitting together at the feet of the Alma Mater ; but he does n't dwell at all on those of us who have been cuddled in her lap. That's what I mean when I say the place is consistently 'American.' " Curtiss got up and took a meditative turn about the room. " The undergraduate body faithfully reproduces, in little, the social orders of the whole country, and not only never formally recognises their existence, but takes occasion, every now and then, somewhat elaborately, to deny it, — a proceeding that of course does n't change any one's position or make any one happier. 'Fine words,' indeed, never ' buttered the parsnips' of so sophisticated a

crowd as you discover at Harvard ; but
if an American community finds it impossible, by reason of all the thousand and
one artificial conditions that make such
things impossible, to be ' free and equal,'
what is left for the distracted concern to
do, but flaunt its freedom and its equality,
from time to time, in theory ? "

"It's all wrong then — frightfully
wrong," declared Hewitt, with considerable
heat. He had been increasingly irritated
through the calm progress of Curtiss's
discourse, and now stood with his back
to the fire-place, staring fixedly before him,
— a spirited figure of protest. "We're
too young at college for that kind of rot,"
he went on emphatically ; " where, in the
name of Heaven, can a fellow expect square
treatment, if it is n't right here among
what, just now, you scornfully called ' a
multitude of lusty young men ' ? They
ought to be too young and too lusty and
too good fellows to care — even to know
about — about — all that." His words
tumbled out noisily, and had the effect
of noticeably increasing Robinson's delib-
erateness.

"The situation would be in no way

remarkable, if it were not for just that fact,
— our extreme youth," Curtiss spoke as if
he were still in college. " It 's taken rather
for granted that young men, who are delightful in so many ways, are the complete embodiment, when chance herds
them together, of the ' hale-fellow-well-
met-God-bless-everybody ' ideal a lot of
people seem to have of them. The plain
truth of the matter is, that at Harvard,
at least, they are n't at all. Wander a
moment from the one royal road we all
try to prance along in common here, and
you 'll find most of us picking our way
in very much the same varied paths we
are destined to follow later on. The only
wonder is that we should have found them
so soon. What makes people's hair stand
on end is that young America should
begin to classify himself so instinctively —
the crystallisation of the social idea
seems, to put it mildly, a trifle premature.
But " — Curtiss's shrug comprehended
many things — " what are you going to
do about it ? "

The question was perfectly general in
intention, and might have ended the discussion had not Hewitt regarded it as

the natural expression of Curtiss's interest in his ambitions for a more diverting existence.

"And yet, after all, I am a gentleman as well as they," he said simply.

There was something exquisitely intelligible to the graduate in the very vagueness of the boy's pronoun. "They," — he too, in the early forlornness of his college life, had been eagerly aware of them, — the great creatures, who, for some reason or other (not always a transparent one), seemed to emerge with such enviable distinction from the vast mediocrity of the crowd; "They" who put on astonishing black coats and spent Sunday afternoon in town; "They" who so frequently wore little crimson usher's badges at the games, and bowed to so many of the attractive people they showed to their seats; "They" who, fine shouldered and brown from rowing on the crews, seemed to endure their education with such splendid listlessness; "They" whom he had so often heard rattling into the suburban stillness of Cambridge just before dawn, from some fine dance in town. How unmistakable they were in the class-room, at a football game, the theatre, — everywhere; how instinctively they seemed to know one another, and how inevitably they came to be felt in every class as something, if not exactly apart, at least aloof.   Curtiss stared musingly at the fire a moment, and smiled as he recalled the various trivial circumstances that, in his own case, gradually, and with none of the excitement of a conscious transition, had brought about the substitution of a perfectly natural, matter-of-fact " We," for the once tacitly understood but exasperating " They."   For a moment he thought of asking Hewitt to explain himself; he had a freakish desire to see the fellow flounder in the effort to be clear, without becoming pitifully transparent; however, he thought better of it, and only answered with some impatience, —

"Of course you 're as much of a gentleman as any one ; but that — except very, very superficially — is n't the question."   Curtiss was beginning to feel like a hoary old oracle.   " There 's nothing strange or tragic in your situation ; it 's shared by lots of other fellows in college," he went on; " you slipped into

Harvard as soon as your tutor thought you were ready to, and, as you came from a rather obscure place, you slipped in quite alone. A year and a half have dragged themselves through the vagaries of the Cambridge climate ; you are still, broadly speaking, quite alone. Yet all this time you have been sensitive — keenly so — to the life that is being lived everywhere around you, and you begin to feel about as essential to the drama as a freshman does when he puts on a somewhat soiled court costume and assists Sir Henry Irving in one of his interesting productions. The trouble with you and every one like you is simply this : you did n't come to Harvard from a preparatory school with a lot of acquaintances and some friends ; you did n't come from any of the few big towns that annually send a number of fellows who know, or who at least have heard, of one another ; you are athletic, perhaps, but scarcely what one would call an athlete — although I confess, that is n't of much consequence ; we don't, as a rule, reward athletes for being athletes. If they perform well, we applaud them. At Harvard, athletics are occasionally a means to a man's becoming identified with the sort of people he wishes to be one of; but I have never known them to be an end.   Finally, you are not a Bostonian, and when I say ' a Bostonian,'" — Curtiss removed his glasses and softly polished them with his handkerchief, — " when I say ' a Bostonian,'" he repeated with the gentlest of satire, " I mean of course a Bostonian that one knows.

" Now, although you are doubtless a great many interesting and attractive things, you do not happen to be any one of those I have just named ; and it is from the men who are, that the crowd destined to be of importance in college — the fellows who are going to lead, who are going to be felt — whatever you choose to call it — will generally originate.   Think of your own class for a moment, and, nine times out of ten, the men that you feel would be congenial as well as interesting, if you knew them, are taken from the sort of men I 've specified."

" Nine times out of ten !" Hewitt laughed hopelessly, " who the devil is the tenth man ? "

"Why, you are, of course, — or you will be," said Curtiss, gaily. "I was myself, once upon a time. It's good fun too ; my little 'boom' was a trifle belated — the tenth man's usually is ; but it only seems to make the more noise for going off all by itself ; while it lasts you almost feel as if people were being superlatively nice to you in order to make up for lost time. Nine times out of ten though " — the sweeping phrase was beginning to assume the dignity of a formula — "it's the other way. The 'tenth man' at Harvard would never have escaped from his obscurity and comparative isolation to become the 'tenth man,' if it were not for something that seems very much like chance."

"How is a fellow going to find his chance in a place like this ? " Hewitt exclaimed scornfully. "Do you suppose, if I knew where to look for it, that I would n't run out to meet it more than half way ? "

"Unfortunately it's the chances that usually seek the introduction," answered Robinson, oracularly.

"You mean to say then, in all seriousness, that a man — a gentleman — who comes here as I did, has no reason to expect that, as a matter of course, his friends will be the kind of people he's been used to at home; that instead of at once finding his own level, he has to sit twirling his thumbs and waiting for the improbable to happen — which it perhaps does n't do in the course of four years?" Hewitt was scornful, incredulous, defiant.

"He is at perfect liberty to hope," said the graduate, quietly; "but I can't see that he has the slightest reason to expect. As for 'twirling his thumbs,' I think he might be better employed if he spent his spare time in going in for foot-ball and glee clubs and the 'Lampoon' and the hundred yards' dash, and all that sort of thing; they bring your name before the college public — make you known and definite, and in that way widen the possibilities."

"Then I can't see that college is very different from any place else — from the outside world," said Hewitt, disappointedly. Curtiss had taken considerable pains to tell him as much some time before; but with Hewitt mere information frequently failed in its mission; he was the sort of

person whom to convince, one was first
obliged to ensnare into believing that he
had arrived at conviction unaided.

"No, it is n't different; that is to say,
Harvard is n't," assented Curtiss; "except that it is smaller, younger and possesses its distinctly local atmosphere."

"Then coming here, under certain circumstances, may be like going to a strange
town and living in a hotel."

"Both ventures have been known to
resemble each other."

"And it 's about as sensible to suppose that your fellow students are going
to take any notice of you, as it would
be to expect people you had never met
to lean out of their front windows and
ask you to dinner if you were to stroll
down the Avenue some fine evening."
Hewitt's manner had become grim and
facetious.

"You seem to have grasped the ele-
ments of the situation," said Curtiss.

"The system is certainly unique,"
mused Hewitt.

"Yes," answered Robinson, "other
colleges have societies; whereas Harvard
unquestionably has Society."

"Do you consider the place snobbish then?" asked Horace.

The graduate thought a moment before answering. "I object to the word," he said at last; "it's as easy to say, as vague and denunciatory, as 'vulgar' or 'selfish' or any of those hardworked terms we apply to other people; you can only say that, making some necessary allowances for a few purely local customs, Harvard society is influenced, or guided, or governed, as you please to express it, by about the same conventions that obtain in other civilised communities. Lots of people who have only a newspaper acquaintance with the place think that wealth is the only requisite here. They have an affection for the phrase 'a rich man's college,' — whatever that may mean. But of course all that is absurd to any one who has spent four years in the place, and has known all the fellows with no allowances to speak of who are welcome in pretty much everything; and has seen all the bemillioned nonentities who languish through college in a sort of richly upholstered isolation. 'Birth' is certainly not the open sesame; a superficial

inquiry into the shop and inn keeping ante-
cedents of some of our most prominent
and altogether charming brothers, smashes
that little illusion. I'm not a sociologist,
and I don't pretend to know what consti-
tutes society with a big S — to put it vulgarly — here or any place else. But there
is such a thing here more than in any
other college. An outsider, hearing me
talk this way, would say I was making an
unnecessarily large mountain out of a very
ordinary molehill. But that's because he
would n't understand that Society at Harvard is really the most important issue
in undergraduate life. The comparatively
few men who compose it, have it in
their power to take hold of anything they
choose to be interested in, and run it according to their own ideas — which shows
the value of even a rather vague form of
organisation. Fortunately, their ideas are
good ones, — clean and manly. You all
find out the truth of this, sooner or later.
Then if you have n't a good time, I suppose you can go away and call the place
snobbish — lots of people do."

"I don't think that's my style exactly,
and I wish you would n't take that tone

about it. I want to know fellows, of
course : fellows like Philip Haydock and
Endicott Davis and Philip Irving and
'Peter' Bradley and Sherman and Prescott," said Hewitt, frankly, naming six of
the most prominent men in his class ; " but
I can't imagine myself thinking - worse
of any of them if — if — "

" If you never do get to know them,"
Curtiss broke in ; " if your chance fails to
materialise — if, after all, you are not the
' tenth man.' " He got up as if to leave.

" I wish you would n't go," said the
other, earnestly ; " there 're lots of things I
want to ask you about. What have men
like Bradley and Davis ever done here to
be what they are ? " he went on hurriedly.

" Ask me something hard," laughed
Curtiss, giving Hewitt his overcoat to hold
for him. " They have n't ' done ' anything," he continued, struggling into his
sleeves; "I don't suppose they would know
how to. Fellows like Bradley and Davis
simply arrive at Harvard when they are
due, to fill, in their characteristic way, the
various pleasant places that have been waiting the last two hundred and fifty years for
them. From the little I 've seen of them, I

should say that these particular two happen to be the kind it would be a pleasure to know anywhere, which is n't always the case with the 'Bradleys' and the 'Davises' of college. So, of course, you want to know them," he ended, emphatically. "What we've been calling your 'chance' literally consists in fellows like these holding out their hands and saying simply, 'Come and see me.'" As Curtiss said this, he impressively extended his own hand; Hewitt shook it, absently, and began with some abruptness to talk of other things.

He was, all at once, exceedingly glad that his guest was saying good-night. It was a positive relief to hear his footsteps resounding in the long corridor outside, and to feel the slight tremor of the building as the massive front door closed with a thump; for Curtiss had become, although perhaps unwillingly, that most objectionable person, the recipient of one's impulsive confidence.

After he had gone, Hewitt stood a moment, looking undecidedly at the glass clock on his mantelpiece. It was long after midnight, and he was in the state of mind when even the oblivion of bed is numbered among sweet but unattainable ambitions. He was tired of his own room ; the good taste that had been expended on it had, of late, begun to strike him as inexpressibly futile. Yet there was scarcely any one on whom he could drop in, even at a reasonable time of night, with the objectless familiarity of college intercourse, to say nothing of calling out under a lighted window in the small hours of the morning. He, of course, belonged to no college club, so his evening expeditions were of necessity limited by the theatres in town, or the listless thoroughfares of Cambridge. He often took long, aimless strolls through streets he barely looked at, and whose names he did n't know. It was with the intention of walking now, that he put on a cap, turned out the lights, and left his room.

The season was that which precedes the first atmospheric intimations of spring. The snow had gone, and the ground was dry, and everything that was shabby and stark and colourless in Cambridge was admitting its inestimable obligation in the past to the loveliness of foliage. There

was little of the sympathetic mystery of
night in the long street in which Hewitt
found himself on leaving his building; its
lines of irregular wooden houses, aggres-
sive with painty reflections of the dazzling
arc-lights swung at intervals overhead,
stretched away in distinct and uninviting
perspective. Except where the gaslit side-
streets yawned murkily down to the river,
Cambridge was hideous in the rectilinear
nakedness of March. The university
town is, as a rule, so very still after twelve
o'clock that its occasional sounds come to
have an individuality to one who prowls
about, that the sounds of day do not possess. Intent as he was in pondering over
the disheartening things Curtiss had been
saying to him, Hewitt's ears were keen, as
he sauntered up the street with his hands
in his pockets, to all the night noises he
had learned to know so well. A student
in a ground-floor room ablaze with light
was reading aloud. Horace stopped a
moment, and laughed at the sleepy voice
droning wearily through the open window, — some one was taking his education
hard. A policeman, half a block ahead of
him, was advancing slowly down the street

by a series of stealthy disappearances into
shadowed doorways; Hewitt could hear
him rattle the doorknobs before he
emerged again to glitter a moment under
the electric light; a car that had left town
at half-past twelve was thumping faintly
along somewhere between Boston and the
Square — it might have been a great dis-
tance away, so intensely still was the inter-
vening suburb; and through all the flat,
silent streets the night air, cool and pun-
gent with the damp of salt marshes, blew
gently up from the Charles and intensified
the atmosphere of emptiness.

Naturally enough, Hewitt's sense of
isolation was far less on these solitary
rambles of his, than when he jostled
elbows in crowded class-rooms with fellows who, he felt, were potentially his
friends, at the same time that he was realising how utterly excluded he was from
their schemes of life. Morbidness was
foreign to a nature like his; and yet, as
time went on, he had been forced to regard
Cambridge as most satisfactory when deserted and asleep. It was only then that
the forlorn feeling of being no essential
part of his surroundings often left him;

and although he recognised the weakness of strolling away from unpleasant truths, the altogether unlooked-for state of affairs at college had cowed him into temporary helplessness. That this furtive condition was temporary, even he himself was in a measure aware; one cannot but feel at college that after a certain time has passed, one's fellows, in spite of the plasticity of youth, become, if not solid, at least viscous, in the moulds that have received them. There is an uneasy period of ebullition in which boys try very hard to enjoy the things that they do, in the absence of the self-poise that enables them to do what they eventually find they enjoy. Intimacies are formed and broken; habits are acquired and not broken; there is a weighing and a levelling, and at last, toward the end of one's sophomore year, almost everybody has been made or marred or overlooked.

It was an intuition of something of this kind that led Hewitt, in his more thoughtful moods, to realise that he was having his worst time now. The great, ill-assorted crowd that technically composed his " class " would shift and change and

finally become, not satisfied, perhaps, with
the various combinations it had evolved,
but certainly used to them.   After that,
life at Harvard, Hewitt told himself, would
be simplified for him; the time for identifying one's self with the companions of
one's choice would have come and gone;
he would find himself standing alone.
His future development would not be
just what he had expected; but there was
peace in the thought that his position
would be definite, unalterable, and then,
after all, he would be standing, and not
running away, as in the past year he had
been so often tempted to do.   Although
anything but a student, he could even
fancy himself ploughing doggedly in self-
defence through an incredible number
of courses in history, or some such subject, and at the end pleasing his family
with two or three Latin words of a lauda-
tory nature on his degree.   Hewitt was
too thinking and too just a person not to
have frequently contrasted his own condition with that of fellows one occasionally heard about, who starved their way
through college on sums that would have
made scarcely an impression on his room-

rent; their persistent "sandiness" compelled his admiration; more than once
he had given substantial expression to it.
But it was at best a very theoretical sort
of consolation that came from a knowledge
of the depressing fact that many of his
most deserving classmates neither ate nor
bathed. His unhappiness differed in kind,
but not in reality.

Although he appreciated how easy and
foolish it was to assume the "chance" the
graduate had dwelt on with such apparent
authority, and then let loose an imagination that had been nourished for so long
on nothing more satisfying than itself,
he, nevertheless, could not help projecting
himself into some of the delightful possibilities of that chance. As he loafed
through sleeping Cambridge, he pictured
himself under a variety of circumstances
playing parts neither fanciful nor egoistic,
but strikingly unlike the one he had been
cast for. The common-place incident of
being joined in the College Yard by two or
three friends on their way to the same
lecture, made his heart beat faster to think
of; the thought of starting off for an
evening in town with a crowd of fellows —

like those talkative groups he so often saw
after dinner, waiting impatiently on the
corner for a bridge car — stirred him to
a mild, pleasant sort of excitement. He
even held imaginary conversations with
Haydock and Davis and Bradley and the
rest of them, in which he modestly refrained from saying all the good things, —
conversations in which these classmates of
his emerged, became individuals, and for
an hour seemed glad to be numbered
among Hewitt's acquaintance. With his
exhaustive knowledge of what might
happen to a boy at college, he liked to
imagine himself in the position where
friends and influence are synonymous,
constantly keeping fresh the memory of
his own dreary experience, and taking
infinite joy in quietly extricating others
from a similar one.

When Hewitt returned to Claverly by
a circuitous way through the College Yard,
and out again into the empty triangular
Square, he found a dumpy, patient-look-
ing herdic cab drawn up to the curbstone.
The driver had tucked away his money
somewhere in the region of his portly
waist, and was pulling his coat over the

spot, preparatory to mounting the box.
But the tall young man in evening dress,
who apparently had just paid him, had
not yet turned to pass through the
brightly lighted doorway. Hewitt, noting
the overcoat that lay limp and unheeded
on the sidewalk, and the almost imperceptible uncertainty of the young fellow's
neat, boyish back in its conscious equilib-
rium, stopped to give that second and
more searching look one always gives a
drunken man, however usual the spectacle
of drunkenness. They both stood there
a moment: Hewitt half way up the stone
steps of the building, the other with his
back turned, swaying gently on the walk
below, as if listening to the diminishing
clatter of the shabby little cab. Horace
scarcely knew why he himself lingered
over an affair so personal and so mani-
festly not his own. He found justifica-
tion for his curiosity, however, — although
it was characteristic neither of his college
nor himself, — when the object of it
started slowly and aimlessly down the
street, leaving his overcoat on the bricks,
where it had dropped.

The garment was a light, slender thing,

and as Horace hung it over his arm and smoothed its soft lining with his fingers, he wondered more what its wearer was like, than what he should do with it. It was easy enough to keep the coat in his room until — as was sure to happen — an advertisement, somewhat vague as to where the article had been lost, appeared in the " Harvard Crimson," or he might restore it at once to its owner, who by this time had stopped undecidedly in the black shadow on the nearest street-corner. There was something companionable in the way the coat clung to his arm, that made him wish to keep it a little longer; but he ended by doing the simpler thing.

" Is n't this your overcoat? " he said, walking up to the sharp line of shadow on the other side of which the shirt bosom and face of the drunken student showed faintly. Hewitt broke the pause that followed by repeating his question.

" Oh, how good of you! I had half decided to go after it," came from the darkness in an astonishingly clear, fresh voice, whose convincing mastery of the first letter of the alphabet left little doubt as to its possessor's birthplace. Had not

the words been said with a formality
that, under the circumstances, was absurd,
Hewitt would have felt that he misjudged
the man's condition.

"Don't mind me, really, I'm very,
very tight." It was impossible to miscon-
strue this statement, or the wild, exultant
over-emphasis with which the final word
was declaimed. Hewitt laughed.

"Oh, are you?" he answered, adding,
"well, here's your overcoat," as if these
two facts existed only in conjunction.

The man in the shadow veered suddenly from the wall he had been leaning
against into the light; and Horace — seeing him distinctly for the first time —
realised that it was his classmate, Bradley.
Coming immediately after the talk with
Curtiss, this meeting was startling to
Horace. It seemed almost prearranged.
He gently forced Bradley to take the
overcoat, said good-night, and turned to
walk away.

"Don't go to bed! Oh, don't go to
bed!" pleaded Bradley, in a sort of en-
gaging whimper. His clutch at Hewitt's
shoulder might have been either a gesture of entreaty or a measure of safety.

"It's early — awf'ly early. The longer
you stay up in Cambridge the earlier it
gets; and the sparrows walk all over
Mount Auburn Street in the morning and
sing, — corking big ones, like ostriches,
— seen them lots of times. Don't go to
bed!"

"I'm afraid I must," said Horace,
looking gravely into his classmate's large,
kindly eyes, that swam helplessly, and
focussed nothing. Bradley took possession of Hewitt's other shoulder; then, in
the intimate confidential tone that for so
long had ceased to exist for Horace, he said,
"I don't want to go to bed — come on!"

The invitation, though as to form rather
indefinite, was most sincere. There was
distinctly some sort of an intention in
Bradley's wish to have the other man
"Come on;" he spoke as if he already
had expressed it. Hewitt, scanning his
drawn face, and then lowering his glance
to the snowy shirt-bosom, tried hard to
find out, without asking, exactly where
"on" was. Of course, any proposition
from the fellow just then might be, in a
general way, safely interpreted, "More
drinks;" instinct told Horace that. But

beyond this broad point of departure,
along what lines did the amiable tipsy
young person intend to proceed? He
was becoming every moment more demon-
strative, more insistent, and by reason of
his condition, rather than in spite of it,
more irresistible. Was he going back to
town? Did he have some stuff in his
own room? Or had he, perhaps, reached
the stage that plans nothing more elaborate than the primitive, genial pastime of
lurching, arm in arm, along the streets and
making a noise? Bradley suddenly answered the unput questions by suggesting
ways and means.

"We can wait until somebody comes
out in a cab, and go back in it; done it
lots of times." He gave Hewitt a little
urging shake.

"Why, you've just come from town
about a minute ago!" Horace's attempt
to back gently from under his friend's
nervous hands was a failure. Bradley
gave him the long, wise look of one whose
mind is blank, until a slow sort of inspiration enabled him to exclaim, —

"Well, you can't stay in there all alone,
can you?" — a very telling bit of argu-

ment. "I came out here to get you; that's why I came out."

Hewitt burst into honest laughter. This tall child struck him as indescribably funny and young and drunk. Then, with a quick downward wriggle, he broke away, still laughing, and made a dash for the steps. Hatless, wild-eyed Bradley, screaming curses into the night, had him round the knees, as he stumbled across the top step to the door. Together they rolled and slid, scuffling, gasping, to the brick sidewalk.

"You would try to get away from me, would you? What a hell of a dirty trick to play a man! You would, would you?"

"Get off my stomach, Bradley, you hurt me."

"You would break away, would you?" The robust emphasis of the remark pounded a painful staccato grunt out of Hewitt's vitals.

"Please let me up!" It took a good deal of self-control to put it just that way; Hewitt had bumped his head, and was beginning to feel the cool bricks against his back.

"Oh, I don't know," mused Bradley, airily; "'you're not the only pebble on the beach.'" Then, after a silence, in which the man under him tried to rest his head more comfortably, "Will you be good? Do you know — I don't think I can trust you! If I let you up, will you do what I want you to?"

"We'll talk it over," the other conceded.

They scrambled to their feet; Hewitt brushed himself off with his cap. Had both men been sober, they would have looked at each other a moment, and laughed. Under the circumstances, the situation was grotesque enough to seem quite natural to Bradley.

"Come on," he said; "now we'll go to town. Oh, my hat! where's my hat — and my coat!" He cursed, as he looked about him, — an amiable, ingenuous ripple of blasphemy, as harmless in intention and as cheerfully spoken as a bit of verse.

A returning cab swung round the corner. Bradley sauntered into the middle of the street to stop it. The manner in which all idea of hat and coat passed from

his mind made Hewitt think of a round-
eyed baby absently letting drop the toy
that has been thrust into its convulsive
little fist. To Horace the cab was an un-
welcome intrusion. He thought it fore-
told complications, and perhaps a scene.
For he had decided, beyond the probability
of changing his mind, that he would not
spend the rest of the night in Boston with
his exhilarated classmate. A nicer reticence than the simple one of moral scruples
kept him from carousing with his new acquaintance. He shrank from taking advantage of this chance — so accidental, so
far-fetched — of impressing himself on the
one fellow in his class whose friendship,
more than any other, he coveted. The
proceeding, he felt, would be a somewhat
thick-skinned one. There was something
in the idea, not quite like winning a
drunken man's money at cards, but suggestive of it. "Peter" Bradley symbolised
to Hewitt an entire chapter of Harvard life.
To-night, Horace felt, in coming so unex-
pectedly on one with whom he existed in
all the intimacy of the imagination, as if he
had been caught surreptitiously reading
the chapter in manuscript.

He went out where Bradley was talking earnestly to the cab-driver.

"Let's not go to town, Bradley," he said, yawning. "It's so far and chilly and everything." Quickly, as if inspired by a new and daring thought, he grasped the boy by the wrist, and exclaimed enthusiastically, "I'll tell you what we'll do — we'll stay in Cambridge!"

"By Heaven, I'll go you! Eh-h-h-h-h-h — we'll stay in Cambridge! we'll stay in Cambridge!" He danced all over the street in a frenzy of mirth and movement, singing again and again, "We'll *stay* in in Cambridge! we'll *stay* in Cambridge! we'll *stay* in Cambridge!" while Hewitt said, "Good-night — sorry he troubled you," to the cabman. A voice from one of the small wooden houses that basks in the shadow of Claverly, yelled, "Oh, shut tup!" very peevishly, just as Bradley threw himself at Horace with a prolonged meaningless scream.

"What do you think you'd like to do now?" asked Hewitt, after a moment, bracing himself to support his burden.

"Wait till I get my breath, and we'll do — everything," panted the burden. It laughed hysterical, extremely silly little laughs. Then solemnly, soberly, Bradley led the way to the curbstone. "Come over here — I want to talk to you; sit down," he said. "Will you wait here and not let a sparrow get by — not a single one — while I dash across and find something to drink?"

"It's getting cold, Bradley; how long will you be?"

"You won't know I've been gone, I'll be so quick." He was off, — half way across the street like a skittish young animal, — then tip-toeing back, stealthy, furtive, mysterious. He crouched by the man on the curbstone, and with his mouth close to Hewitt's ear whispered earnestly : —

"If I tell you something, will you promise not to tell? It's a secret, you know."

"I don't think you'd better," gravely.

"I must, — it's killing me."

Horace looked to see if the fellow was crying.

"I'll never repeat it to any one," he promised.

"It's awful, — horrible," moaned Brad-

ley, drawing closer to Hewitt, and putting
his arms round him. "It's this," he
sobbed; "I don't believe in either Space
or Time." He was gone again, with a
backward spring that sent the other
sprawling. Horace sat up and watched
the boy dart across to an opposite house,
fumble a moment at the door, and dis-
appear with a slam. Instantly every window upstairs and down glowed yellow.
The noise of a piano, slapped pettishly
from bass to treble by an open palm,
came over to the young man who sat
thinking on the curbstone.

What he thought was just about what
any other normal person, under the same
circumstances, would have thought. He
wondered how long it would be before
Peter came back; what they would do
when he did come back; and where that
night was leading. It might take him,
Horace, far, — almost anywhere, — away
from himself, to a troop of friends, to
the club across the street. Or it might
leave him at night's ordinary desti-
nation. But whatever the end, the beginning was his opening, his chance. It
had pranced at him in the guise of a crazy,

faunlike, drunken thing; thanks to Curtiss, he had recognised it.

He tried to picture to himself the inside of the club house, over whose charmed threshold his friend had just plunged. He also marvelled a moment at the vagaries of inebriety; it was curious, for instance, that any one so far gone — so driven by every whimsical, erratic impulse as Bradley — should give heed to the etiquette that did not permit him to take into the club a man who had no club of his own. How artful the youth must have thought himself, when he left Horace behind, ostensibly to detain any large imaginary sparrows that might pass that way. Hewitt had begun to hope that the drink Bradley brought back might be beer, when the windows opposite blackened, the door slammed, and the boy came toward him once more. His expedition had not been in vain; in one hand he carried a pompous looking bottle, in the other some glasses that clinked cheerfully as he walked. From under one of his arms a second bottle aimed at Hewitt like a small piece of artillery.

"Unload me. That one's burgundy;

look out, don't spill it, I pulled the cork.
The other's fizz. These are glasses.
Got a knife? — cut the wires." Bradley
sat down on the curbstone.

"This looks as if we were going to see
the sunrise," said Hewitt, opening his
penknife.

"I'd rather wait till hell freezes over;
seen the other thing lots of times." He
filled a long glass more than half full
of burgundy, and guzzled it. "Ugh —
what belly wash — hot as tea."

"That's what you get for looking on
the wine when it's red. Here — try this."
Hewitt handed the other glass. It foamed
at the edges.

"I could die drinking this stuff," said
Bradley, fervently.

"You probably will — here, give me
some." Horace with difficulty got possession of the glass, and held it to his lips.
Bradley amused himself by wiping his
wet hands in his friend's hair.

They sat there until Peter had managed to drink and spill the contents of
both bottles. He refused to tell where
his room was, so Hewitt attempted to
take him to Claverly. The task called

for an infinite amount of patience and
tact as well as time.   For Peter's manner,
though all at once excessively polite, was
firm.

"It's ever so good of you to take all
this trouble for me," he asserted, in worried tones.   Then he would lie down in
the street, saying he was a dead horse,
and refuse to get up.   The affair became almost annoying when, on reaching
the inside of Claverly by a great number
of almost imperceptible advances, Bradley tore the fire apparatus from its red
cage on the wall in one of the long corridors, and screamed "Fire!" like a
maniac.   If anything in the situation
admitted of being called fortunate, it was
the proximity of Horace's room at that
particular moment.

The proctors in Claverly are supposed
to sleep in the attitude of one whose
ears are tense with listening.   And it has
been said that during the hours in which
convention prescribes pyjamas, their costume is of blanket wrappers and felt slip-
pers.   Their appearance upon a "scene
of disturbance" has been estimated, vari-
ously, as simultaneous with the disturb-

ance, or anywhere from one to ten seconds after it. Horace had just time enough to thrust Peter into his room, lock the door, and begin to gather up the hose, when Mr. Tush — arriving silently from nowhere — was there. The dishevelled Mr. Tush was absurd or sublime, according to the mood of the one who apperceived him. To the dispassionate onlooker, he merely gave an impression of hair and responsibility.

"The janitor will arrange the fire apparatus, Mr. Hewitt," he said, drily. "By the way, would you mind explaining why it happens to be on the floor?"

Hewitt did explain. He was very sorry; a friend of his had come out from town; the friend was not quite himself; he was noisy and unmanageable; it would not happen again.

"There has been a great deal of disturbance in the building recently, Mr. Hewitt."

Horace could think of no answer in which impertinence did not lurk.

"Where is your friend?"

"In my room."

"Is he a student in Harvard University?"

" No."

" Good-night, Mr. Hewitt."

" Good-night, Mr. Tush."

Afterward, whenever Hewitt thought over his meeting with Peter Bradley, the monosyllable loomed up big and disconcerting. What preceded and followed it were nothing. He had not minded Bradley's drunken tyranny; the experience was novel. He had not objected to undressing the boy and putting him to bed; it was inevitable. But the lie meant something, and the memory of it hurt; although he believed it to be the simplest, most effective way of disposing of Tush.

Hewitt spent what was left of the night on his divan, and got up in time for a nine o'clock. He would have much rather slept until noon; but he did not want to be in his room when Bradley woke; he felt it might be rather trying for Bradley. So he hung clean towels over the edge of the bathtub, and pinned a note to the back of the chair on which he had laid his guest's clothes, saying: " Sorry I have to run away. Hope you 'll find everything you want." It was after eleven o'clock when he came

back; but the fellow was still sleeping.
Horace stood in the doorway a moment
and watched the flushed, childish face
on the pillow; it seemed incredible that
Peter should be curled up there in bed.
Then he tiptoed away and had luncheon
at a hotel in town, and spent the afternoon looking at shop-windows.

Three days afterwards, while Hewitt
was waiting in his room for Curtiss, who
was coming round for a walk, Bradley
came to see him. It was probably not a
very easy thing to do; but Bradley did it
adequately. His manner — sober — was
the kind that a stranger attributes to shyness, an intimate friend to simplicity.

"I was n't nice at all the other night,
was I?" he said, after a moment of awk-
wardness, during which they both laughed.
"I 'm awfully sorry about it really; it
must have bored you like anything.".

"It did n't at all," declared Horace.
He held out a package of cigarettes.

"Well, tell me what happened; I
think I must have been a great deal
tighter than you thought I was."

"No, I don't think that —" began
Hewitt, at which they laughed some

4

more. "Why, nothing very much happened; you merely — do you remember getting the champagne and burgundy?"

"Oh, perfectly."

"Well, do you remember lying down in
the street and refusing to get up?"

"No-o-o — " very doubtfully. (After
all, I suppose one does n't remember such
things.)

"Well, you did, and I had a time getting you here; and don't you remember
anything at all about the hose and the
proctor and— "

So it was lived over again from beginning to end, with a great deal of detail and
laughing and remorse of a cheerful and
unconvincing kind. Bradley looked serious when he heard the part about the
proctor; but on learning that Mr. Tush
had not seen him, and that Hewitt's lie
had made the chance of a more careful inquiry quite improbable, he found the
whole thing immensely amusing.

"I have a lot to thank you for," he
said, staring about the room. Hewitt
made the inevitable protest, and then
there was a pause. These two persons,

who were Harvard men, classmates, and about the same age, suddenly had nothing to talk about. The single point at which their lives touched was the tiniest dot on the page of their experience, — the sort of dot, too, that both were willing to ignore as quickly as possible. They no doubt listened to the same lectures from time to time. But one does not, apropos of nothing at all, discuss the Malthusian Doctrine or the importance of the semicolon in literature.

You can't talk to a college man about himself, when his career is a pleasanter one than your own, because — well, because you must n't. And you can't talk to a man who is to you an unknown quantity, — a nonentity, a cipher, — simply because you can't. It's all very distressing, and you talk about athletics. But in the month of March the effort is transparent and a bore. Neither football nor base-ball is contemporaneous; the crew is still rather vague; and when you plunge recklessly into track athletics, it occurs to you, all at once, that you have n't taken the trouble to go near any since your freshman year. It's impos-

sible, therefore, to recall whether Spavins
is the person who ran the hurdles in sixteen, or reached incredible heights in the
pole vault; it is even likely that Spavins
did neither, and was all the time behind
the bleachers absorbed in putting the
shot.   To tell the truth, you don't know
Spavins ;   you   have   never   met   him ;
you never will, and you always skip the
column in the " Crimson " that records his
exploits.

This was the basis on which Hewitt
and Bradley finished their talk.   The peculiar occasion of their being in the same
room together was at an end.   Bradley
lingered merely because an innate sense of
proportion kept him there ; to leave the
minute you say the only thing you came
to say, is like running out of church before
the people all round you are done confid-
ing things to the backs of the pews in
front of them.   Your devotions only
properly cease when the subdued spontaneous exertion of stout women regaining
the perpendicular gives you the signal.
Bradley was waiting for the signal.   The
bell on Harvard Hall, calling students to
the last lecture of the day, sounded it.

" There goes the bell; I must hurry along," he said, fingering the note-book he had brought with him.

" Oh, cut your lecture ! " came from Horace rather eagerly. Bradley looked up in surprise. His face was not well fashioned for concealing what went on in his head. Just now it distinctly said, " How extraordinary ! Why should I cut my lecture ? " His words, however, were, " Oh, no, thank you ; I must run along ! " He took another cigarette to smoke on the way over to the Yard, and sauntered round the room, although he mentioned more than once his fear of being late. At the door, he turned to say, " Well, good-bye ; I hope you know how much obliged I am to you for all that."

" There is n't anything really. Good-bye." Horace assisted at the opening and shutting of the door, in the unnecessary way one does with strangers. Then he walked slowly up and down his study, with his hands in his pockets, whistling energetically under his breath, and stopping every now and then to stare out of the window. Curtiss came in almost immediately.

" I met that good-looking classmate of
yours, Bradley, at the door," he said.
Curtiss walked straight up to Hewitt, — he
had a dramatic way of doing almost everything, — and grasped his friend's hand.
" Has he been here?" he asked, smiling
a pleased smile.

" Yes; he's just left."

A pause.

" Did he ask you to go see him?"

" No," very simply.

" Will he come back?"

" No."

" The pig!"

" I beg your pardon, he's nothing of
the kind."

" I'm afraid I don't understand, then."

" Oh, yes, you do, better than anybody,
except possibly myself."

Another silence.

" Well, go on; I'm waiting."

" Why should the man ask me to go
see him?" asked Hewitt, passionately.
" He—"

" But, my dear boy!" protested Curtiss.

" Don't! don't!" Horace drew away
pettishly. " When you bluff like that,
you make me sick. Bradley has done

everything he ought to have done, and
more too," he went on quietly. " If I
expect more, I'm a fool; if you do,
you 're a hypocrite! Bradley might have
written me a polite note, and considered
the thing square. Instead of that he took
the trouble to climb up here to apologise
and thank me. He was well-bred and
polite and unget-at-able, — the way gentlemen ought to be. And that 's all; that 's
the end of it. We 'll never see each
other again; why should we? I suppose if I 'd gone to any other college
in the country, and this had happened,
Bradley would have put his paws on my
shoulders and lapped my face; and we 'd
have roomed together next year, and proposed to each other's sisters on Class Day.
But I did n't go to any other college;
I 'm damned glad I did n't, — everybody
always is. I don't know why, but I am.
Between you and Bradley, I 've learned
more about this place than I ever knew
there was to know. If I could write, I 'd
knock the spots out of any magazine
article on Harvard that 's ever been
printed." Horace stopped and looked
out of the window. What he had been

saying was a curious mixture of bitterness
and indifference.

"Come, let's take a walk," he exclaimed briskly, in another tone.

"Yes, let's," answered Curtiss; "that's
what I came for," and he began to hum,
while Horace was looking for a hat, —

> "Oh, Harvard was old Harvard
> When — "

THE SERPENT'S TOOTH

"COLLEGE life," murmur old men, as they pause a moment, before getting into bed, and listen to the singing of some drunken cabmen in the street below.

"College life," whisper the Cambridge unsought, as they cut out preposterous baby clothes at the Social Union and discuss somebody or other's ungraceful departure from the University.

"College life," shudder apprehensive mothers, diagnosing the athletic column for dislocations.

"College life," mutters the father of the man who got sixteen A's and brain fever.

"College life" — but Dickey Dawson and the three fellows who had stopped in to see him that afternoon, rather prided themselves on not being typical of any recognised phase of that comprehensive platitude. They had all, thus far, in their

college life, ingeniously escaped going in
for anything in particular and were in the
habit of regarding themselves as a nucleus
for a future society, to be composed of
unrepresentative Harvard men. Little
Dickey Dawson even went so far as to
be almost ashamed of his own undeniable
popularity; but, as he remarked apologetically, " It is not always possible to
avert success."

He was not well that afternoon. The
college physician had come, caused
Dickey to throw back his head, open
wide his mouth and say " ah-h-h, ah-h-h,"
while he peered in with a sort of depreca-
tory craftiness and found, " no white
spots, but a state of congestion."

Generally speaking, your acquaintances
at college do not realise that you have
been sick until they meet you in the
Yard and are given an opportunity to
express their belated sympathy. The
men, however, who were gossiping in
Dickey Dawson's room that day, were the
men who had missed him at breakfast and
luncheon and had come to hunt him up
— the men, in short, whom he knew best
and enjoyed most.

There was Tommy, with the profile and the glasses. He was the sort of person who occasionally writes wordy little book reviews for an obscure literary magazine, and refers to himself, now and then, as " a driven penny-a-liner." Then there was Charlie Bolo who was not popularly credited with much sense beyond his exceedingly deformed sense of humour. There was also Bigelow — a bore with an accomplishment. All three of them had a kind of verbal agility that passed, among themselves, for cleverness.

"What means this ghastly pomp and circumstance?" asked Dickey Dawson from the sofa, as he reached out and clutched at the voluminous tails of Tommy's frock coat.

"It means, my dear, that I have been to see two women whom I never met before," answered Tommy, daintily gathering his skirts about him and sitting down. "One of them lived in a suburb and was perfectly horrible."

"The other," put in Charlie Bolo, who possessed the disagreeable gift of conversational prophecy, "lived in a dungeon on

a proper street, and was merely horribly
perfect."

"Yes, you are right," assented Tommy,
complacently. "She was a Bodkin, and —
well — you know — Bodkins are Bodkins." He submitted to the *sui generical*
fashion in which one is obliged to refer to
certain Boston families.

"Ah, you know a Bodkin, you know
the kind of woman I mean," he went on
dramatically. "She's the woman who
lies awake at night — dreading your arrival, for her only clew to your identity is
a perfunctory letter of introduction in-
forming her that you are from a place of
which she never heard. She is the
woman who, when you call, roosts discreetly at the extreme end of a long sofa
and extends a series of well-worn social
'feelers,' while her daughter makes tea
in a masterly, unemotional way, and sup-
poses, from time to time, 'that you graduate this year,' or 'that you must find
Cambridge dull after — after — '"

"Those are some of the local formulae
for tact," broke in Charlie Bolo.

"The other one — the suburban — was
truly a most loathely creature," continued

Tommy in the harsh incisive voice that made what he said so difficult to forget. " She did n't even give me tea ; and you know how many clever things I can say about tea." His smile was an impertinent challenge. " My Aunt got me into it," he half yawned ; " there was, I believe, some reason why I ought to go, and as it was n't a very urgent one — I went. The thing actually seemed glad to see me."

" Imagine," laughed Dickey Dawson cautiously, for he was learning how to regulate his spontaneity when talking to fellows like Tommy and Charlie Bolo and Bigelow, and had come to believe that he laughs best who laughs least.

" Yes, and she 'd been abroad and seen the Passion Play, or the Lakes of Killarney, or some such thing, and was altogether a most impossible sort of a person. I fancy she is what they call ' a superior woman ' in this country — they don't exist anywhere else, I believe."

Dickey Dawson's throat was too sore to admit of his talking much himself, and as Tommy was there to entertain him he said :

" Curse her more specifically."

"Oh, what is the use?" Tommy shrugged his shoulders. "Besides, I could n't very well, as the superior woman is not a human being, but a type. You 've certainly seen lots of her — there is no man fortunate enough not to have. They appeal to the imagination of —"

"Of the unimaginative, who always marry them," interrupted Charlie Bolo.

"Yes, and are n't they usually stout, or inclined to be?" asked Bigelow, abstractedly. He was looking through some music books at the piano.

"Oh dear yes; no thin woman need aspire to superiority, nor no unmarried one either. They are essentially wives and mothers, but not vulgarly so necessarily." It was what he considered accuracy rather than any latent charity that had induced Tommy to add this detail.

"A woman whose efficiency transcends every emergency, known or unknown, is in a fair way toward becoming superior," he continued. "She 's the abnormally normal — the hope of the race — the oatmeal of humanity — *Philistia felix* — wow!"

Charlie Bolo had a habit, not uncom-

mon among college men in college rooms,
of carrying on most of his conversation
with his back turned, and at the same
time examining minutely every picture in
the apartment, vaguely opening most of
the books and putting them down again,
critically peering at a " shingle " here, and
striking a meaningless chord or two on
the piano there, and from time to time
asking questions about one's various be-
longings, answers to which — if ever rashly
undertaken — involved the short but intricate history of one's life.   Charlie Bolo,
who from an extended practice in doing
all these depressing things had reduced
his method of inspecting a room to a sort
of erratic system, was just finishing the
third wall and passing on to the mantelpiece of Dickey Dawson's study.   Here
he stopped to admire, for the hundredth
time or more, a picture of Dawson's
mother.   Simultaneously Tommy came to
the end of his wordy little diatribe, and
glanced up with what was known to the
others as his most " receptive smile." He,
too, seemed to suspend animation before
Mrs. Dawson's likeness, and during the
second or two of silence that followed,

both Bigelow and Dickey found their at-
tentions fixed on the picture that Charlie
Bolo had taken in his hand.

Mrs. Dawson, a remarkably young-
looking woman in evening dress, was leaning slightly back in one of the massive,
richly carved chairs peculiar to ancient
Italy and modern photography.

From the point of view of mere line
Mrs. Dawson seemed to be a handsome
woman.   However, it was not the manner in which her somewhat haughty head
stood out from the soft, dull grey of its
tapestry background, nor yet the white
slope of her shoulders against the dark
wood, that most impressed one.   The
charm of the picture — for it unquestionably had great charm — came rather from
the perfection of the lady's equipment,
and the regal ease with which she seemed
to ignore it.   Charlie Bolo, who had the
wisdom of a man with sisters, always
found the photograph of Mrs. Dawson
faultless — from the bit of white ribbon
twisted through her hair, and the fan of
ostrich plumes, and the long, limp glove
lying lightly across her lap, to the non-
committal exposure of shoe-tip.

There was the briefest possible pause in the talk; but coming at the exact time it did, it was more than long enough to enlighten every one as to what every one else was thinking. To Dickey Dawson, who seized the opportunity of giving all three men a hasty, apprehensive glance, it was as if some one had in so many words exclaimed, " At least this woman is not superior ! "   But, of course, no one could have exclaimed such a thing with Tommy sitting there, exerting the tacit admonition of inspired refinement.

This tribute, manifesting itself in spontaneous silence, was fraught with both pleasure and wretchedness for Dickey Dawson: pleasure, that these fellows whom he so admired and looked up to, should unquestioningly accept the splendid picture lady as his mother, together with all that the relationship implied; wretchedness, because he was much too intelligent a young person not to be thoroughly aware that the splendid picture lady was a glorified arrangement of upholstery and apparel, bearing about as much resemblance to his mother as, for purely decorative purposes, he chose to have it bear.   He was proud

of the portrait, because it was a success of
his own conceiving; he loathed it, because
it was forever rubbing in the fact that his
relations, though doubtless admirable in
the exercise of their respective domestic
functions, were execrable as a social background. He detested it also, because it
kept unpleasantly vivid in his mind the
long diplomatic struggle that had preceded its taking.

"Other boys have family pictures in
their rooms at college," he had said to
his mother in the vacation that followed
his sophomore year; "I want one of you
to take back with me." Whereupon Mrs.
Dawson, with considerable pleasure and
some reminiscent vanity, had produced
several from an album. Dickey had inspected them gravely, from the one in
which his mother was picking shamelessly
artificial pond-lilies over the side of an
unseaworthy skiff, to the jauntily posed
"cabinet size."

"I should like to have one that looked
more as you do now," he had said, affec-
tionately smoothing her hair and wondering if he could manage it.

He had managed it, of course. He was

always tactful, and could on occasions be tender and persuasive. These qualities, added to the authority he exerted in his capacity of American child, had in time overcome his mother's objections to the background, properties, pose, coiffure, and, most difficult of all, the costume he had insisted on — had, in fact, even achieved a sublime finishing touch by having, instead of an ordinary gilt advertisement, the pliable photographer's name scrawled carelessly in pencil across the margin of his print. Mrs. Dawson had been exceedingly shocked at the result, and had, not unnaturally, failed to recognise herself in the gracious, self-possessed personage who gave one the impression of having sunk into that picturesque seat for a moment, until her carriage should be called. She had speedily regretted, what she from time to time referred to as her "weakness," and had hastened to exhibit the strength she still retained by breaking the negative with her own hands — not, however, before Dickey had procured some striking proofs of it. The very success of the picture was what made it such a disturbing addition to Dawson's room. In the appreciation of his friends it had furnished him with precisely the sort of mother to which his eclectic and exotic inclinations seemed to entitle him. He himself, in his more placid moods, derived an indefinable satisfaction from the thing, and was in the habit of sitting before it, musing contentedly on his perfect adaptability to the people and surroundings he had never been used to at home — an adaptability that sometimes caused him to wonder whether he were not, after all, illegitimate or adopted. Ordinarily, however, this fanciful parent of his appeared to him in the light of a cunningly devised, automatic lie that kept on telling itself to make him miserable.

Charlie Bolo carefully returned the photograph to its place. His back had been turned to the room and he was, perhaps, the only one of the four men who did not realise the direction every one's thoughts had taken.

"I think I shall have to get rid of that libel on my mother," mused Dawson, brazenly.

"I was so sorry not to find Mrs. Dawson in the afternoon I called," said Char-

lie Bolo, passing on to a silver candlestick.
" Is she to be long in town ? "

" So was I," murmured Bigelow ; " Bolo
and I went together."

"You must give her a tea," suggested
Tommy, getting up. When he had on
his frock coat, he sat intermittently.

" I should like to, tremendously," lied
Dawson, with a pleasant smile ; " but you
see she's going away to-morrow. She was
awfully cut up about missing you fellows —
I think she was at a luncheon, or some such
thing." He courageously took the chances
of any one's having seen her naïvely ad-
miring the Washington Elm and the Long-
fellow House on the afternoon in question.
" She's going to be here such a very short
time " — this was a detail, but it seemed
just as well to dwell on it — " that you
can fancy how I feel about being laid up
like this."

Bigelow said, " rotten," or some equally
piquant idiom of assent, and Charlie Bolo,
by commenting technically on a Dutch tile
he had come across, was on the point of
giving an entirely new turn to the talk,
when something happened.

It has often been told how little Dickey

Dawson, once upon a time, saved somebody or other's life by coolly dangling
himself to the bridle of a big, runaway
horse. The occasion on which he drew
red hot poker sketches where a dog had
bitten the calf of his leg, has likewise had
its historians. But no one has ever described what took place when, in the midst
of Charlie Bolo's exposition of tile paint-
ing, Dickey called, "Come in!" to a
doubting knock at the door, and Mrs.
Dawson advanced two steps into the study
and then stopped.

For a moment no one, with the exception of Dawson, grasped the situation.
He had grasped it and was wrestling with
it as he threw off the rug that covered him
where he lay on the sofa — as he stepped
across the room — as he placed his hands
on his mother's shoulders and kissed her
lightly on the cheek. He had grasped
the situation, but he was utterly at a loss
to know what to do with it.

"Did n't you get my telegram?" his
mother was saying; "why, that's funny —
I sent one from the hotel quite a time ago,
'Am worried about sore throat will come
to see you' — just ten words exactly."

Then he found himself introducing his three friends to her : Tommy first, Charlie Bolo second, and Bigelow last, and as he pronounced their names slowly and distinctly, he tried to look ahead and discover what he should do next.

On realising that the impassive Tommy was being presented to her, Mrs. Dawson began to extend her hand toward him ; but her impulse collapsed for some reason or other and the movement resulted in nothing more definite than the disclosure of her silk mits.

The three men were so completely outside of any calculations she had made before knocking on her son's door, that she had nothing to say to them just then, so she turned once more to Dickey with frank adoration and said, —

" I *was* worried about your throat."

" I suppose, like the rest of us, Mrs. Dawson, you have found out how seriously he objects to the serious," ventured Charlie Bolo airily. The smile Mrs. Dawson gave him did not lack sweetness, for she had been looking at Dickey ; but it was desperately vague, and Bolo felt that he had made a false start.

"They are taking pretty good care of me, don't you think?" There was something pallid and heroic about Dickey's playfulness.

"Oh, this college life!" began Mrs. Dawson, forgetfully. She was trying to recollect a clipping she had once made from a newspaper.

"There's a lack of woman's sweeping, without doubt," grumbled Bigelow jocosely — the music books he had been examining had dirtied his hands.

"Richard, what was that piece I cut from the 'Weekly' and sent you last year?" Mrs. Dawson sat down in the chair Dickey pushed toward her. It was a heavy chair of dark wood, and gave Tommy a vicious desire to look at the picture on the mantelpiece. Dickey elaborated the little anecdote to which his mother referred and made the most of it — it was nearly dinner time; the fellows would certainly go soon.

"You have so many books, Richard," said Mrs. Dawson, looking about the room for the first time.

"Are n't his shelves attractive," assented Tommy with enthusiasm. "I think you

would approve of everything there too,
Mrs. Dawson, with the possible exception
of this, which you undoubtedly know
enough about to disapprove of." He
laughingly handed her a volume of " Degeneration " from the table. Dawson
could have slain him had he not realised
that all three fellows must be somewhat
bewildered.

" Is n't it — is n't it — thick — " faltered
Mrs. Dawson.

" What *is* one to think of a creature
like Nordau ? " asked Bigelow, theatrically ;
" that is to say, of course, beyond his exquisitely unconscious sense of humour."
He had made this remark on several
previous occasions, and its technique was,
in consequence, becoming quite perfect.
Mrs. Dawson looked helplessly at Dickey
and said nothing. She was at least dis-
playing what Charlie Bolo called " admirable *savoir taire.*"

When she opened the volume and
leaned over to examine the title-page,
Tommy gave the photograph on the
mantelpiece a surreptitious glance. There
was a more or less grotesque resemblance
in it to the almost portly, middle-aged

original, who was dressed with a quiet
absence of taste and answered in a general
way Tommy's description of a superior
woman. It was very embarrassing and
inexplicable and altogether impossible.
Tommy did not understand it — he did
not understand anything any more, and
only wished to get outside and pinch himself and Charley Bolo and Bigelow.

Dickey Dawson did most of the talking,
and achieved thereby a dismal sort of success. His mother had introduced — or
rather stumbled on — fallen over — the
subject of books, and for a time it was as
if Dawson had said to himself, —

" Books ! books ! what can I say of the
origin, development, history, and present
condition of books ? " For he chattered
incessantly about them — his own — Tommy's — anybody's. He told funny stories
that were not in the least funny, about book
agents, and was in the midst of a detailed description of a book-case when he realised he
was making a fool of himself and stopped.

" I like reading," mused Mrs. Dawson,
as she mechanically turned the leaves of
" Degeneration."   " I think it cultivates
the observation."

" I feel sometimes that it would be more advisable to cultivate blindness than observation," answered Tommy. He was becoming reckless and got up to go.

Mrs. Dawson's lips parted to say something, but Dickey broke in with, —

" I wish one of you fellows would kindly stop at the stable and send round a cab. It is too late for my mother to go back to town in the car."

A protest from Mrs. Dawson seemed imminent, but she apparently thought better of it and returned to the book.

The getting away was difficult, but not nearly so difficult as staying any longer would have been. They chirped " good-byes," and " get well soons," and " so glad to have met yous," galore, and Bigelow felt waxing within him a new and passionate love for his own family, who were all decently dead. Then they echoed off through a long corridor. After they had gone Mrs. Dawson said nothing for several minutes, and Dickey made a noise with the fire.

" They 're queer young men," she finally reflected aloud. " Do you like them very much, Richard?"

"Oh, yes," answered Dickey, indifferently, "you get to like people you see a great deal, I imagine." He sat on the arm of his mother's chair and held one of his mother's hands and kissed it.

"I wonder if you get to *dis*like people you *don't* see much of," said Mrs. Dawson. She was turning the leaves of her book without stopping to look at them.

"Not if you ever truly loved them," answered Dickey, tenderly drawing nearer to her and laying his cheek against hers. He was almost overdoing the thing.

"Not if you ever truly loved them, I suppose," thoughtfully repeated his mother with more intelligence than Dickey had ever given her credit for.

Then she began to turn the leaves of the book all over again.

WOLCOTT THE MAGNIFICENT

I

IN some way or other it came to the notice of Barrows, the Recording Secretary, that Ernest McGaw was literally starving. The Secretary, being a person of appreciation, immediately gave the man food.

"I'm a horribly busy creature," he said to McGaw; "but if you'll come round to dinner with me at the Colonial Club this evening, we can talk about things." Of course McGaw went and dined — for the first time in months; for two weeks he had been keeping himself half alive on oatmeal that he cooked in a shallow tin apparatus, over the lamp he studied by.

The Secretary had ridden a bicycle that afternoon, and seemed half famished himself, which soothed McGaw's raw, quivering sensibilities from the first. Then,

besides, Barrows was probably the most
genial, natural, receptive, unacademic person that ever answered to an official name.
So afterwards, when they went into an
unoccupied room upstairs, and the Secretary smoked a cigar, it was more than
easy — it was comforting — for McGaw
to tell him the whole squalid little trag-
edy. There was nothing particularly new
in it to the Secretary, since he was a gentleman who spent his life in making the
struggle easier for men who tried to go
through college with a capital consisting
of fourteen cents and a laudable ambition.
Youth and bitterness in combination were
some of the materials he dealt in. Barrows could have told the story of Mc-
Gaw's pinched, colourless existence much
better than McGaw could ; yet for an
hour or more he listened, questioned, dis-
cussed, and was moved. Later, when he
and McGaw parted in the Yard, the Secretary, before going to bed, wrote a carefully thought-out letter to Sears Wolcott
2nd, of the sophomore class.

Sears Wolcott got the letter the next
evening, when he stopped a moment in
Claverly, on his way from the training

table to his club, — that is to say, to one
of his clubs. He was a member of two,
besides, naturally, the Institute, of whose
privileges, by the way, he rarely availed
himself. After dining at the training table with his class crew, he usually dropped
in at his nearest club to smoke the one
pipeful allowed him by his captain. To-
night, however, Barrows' letter put him in
such a bad temper that he forgot about
his pipe, looked sullen, and spoke to no
one. Wolcott was a very big boy; when
he was angry, he seemed to swell and swell
until everything in the vicinity got out of
drawing. Nobody but Haydock had
even noticed him come in; the others
were too absorbed in drinking their coffee and chattering about the class races.
Haydock's greeting, "How is The Magnificent One this evening?" did not meet
with the reception that encourages further
pleasantries. Haydock was the only
other man in the club who was not talking as fast and as loud as he knew how.
But his quiet was as different from The
Magnificent One's as the placid stillness
of a summer evening differs from the
awful silence in which one waits for a fun-

nel-shaped cloud to mature. Haydock
had a big cigar in one hand and a little
coffee-cup in the other. He was thinking that a good room in a good club,
with its dark walls, and all its leather
chairs and divans and rugs, with its
magazines and convenient lights to read
them by, with its absence of personal
individuality, was, especially just after dinner, the most satisfactory spot in the
world. Even the background of cheerful
noise was agreeable. "As long as you 're
not called on to help make it," added
Haydock to himself, as one of the talkers
detached himself from the others, and,
flourishing a paper in his face, called
out : —

"Who wants to subscribe to the Prospect Union ?"

Wolcott reached for the nearest newspaper, and buried himself in it; he could n't
endure Ellis.

"Who wants to subscribe to the Pros-
pect Union? Only a dollar," repeated
Ellis, wiggling his subscription list before
Wolcott's eyes.

"What the devil is the Prospect
Union?" growled Wolcott. He crum-

pled the " Transcript " and tossed it back
on the table.

"Why, don't you know?" asked Ellis,
in genuine surprise.   "I've taught geog-
raphy there for two years."

Wolcott snapped back a single word.
It was neither a pretty word nor a refined
one; the mildest significance one could
attach to it was that Wolcott was scarcely
in sympathy with Ellis or anything that
was his.

"The Prospect Union," explained
Haydock, in the deliberate way that was
so often taken seriously, "is a most admirable educational institution, carried on in
Cambridgeport by the Harvard undergraduate. It is elaborately designed to
make the lower classes — the labouring
man — dissatisfied with his station in life.
I am proud to say, that I once went there
every Friday night for six months to teach
two bricklayers, three dry-goods clerks,
and a nigger how to appreciate the beautiful works of the late Mr. Keats. I
spoiled their lives, and they all love me.
Allow me, in my humble way, to help
the cause." He rolled a silver dollar the
length of the table to Ellis. Ellis smiled,

and put the money in his pocket; he considered Haydock a very "unmoral" person indeed, but liked him, and hoped that some day he would make something of himself.

"That's very nice — now who's the next patron?" the philanthropist went on, earnestly. "The Prospect Union is really a mighty fine thing. Even if the men down there don't learn very much out of books, they can come there and see us," he had almost unnoticeably emphasised the "us."

"My God!" said Wolcott, slowly. The words and the way he sized up Ellis, from top to toe, were heavy with a sort of thick-headed contempt. "They can go there and look at *you*, can they?" Wolcott muttered the unrefined word again. Then he got up with an enormous stretch, yawned, looked at Ellis once more, and laughed, as he went out of the room.

Of the lesser brutalities, a contemptuous laugh is, perhaps, the most brutal of all. Ellis's thin face reddened. There was silence until the outer door slammed.

"Damn such a man!" declared Ellis, in a loud whisper. This was bold language for him to speak. Later in the night, he woke up and thought about it.

"Oh, I would n't," protested Haydock, mildly. "He's so magnificent."

"Well, I can't see it!" Ellis was smarting; but he could n't relieve himself with the appropriate sharp retort; it did n't come to him until later on, in bed. "No one has any right to be such a hog, — especially in a club. Besides, I was n't talking to him in particular. He need n't have subscribed, if he did n't want to; I never expected he would, although almost every one else has. What's a dollar anyhow?" he shrugged his shoulders.

"Yes, what is it?" piped a tiny person, trying to relieve the tension, from the other side of the table. "I have n't seen one since the first of last February."

"No, but seriously," demanded Ellis, — he was always demanding something seriously, — "what do you think of a man who does things like that, not only once, but every day — all the time?"

"Well, what did he do?" Haydock was never unprepared to take the other side of any argument in which Ellis engaged. "In the first place, he came into

the club so quietly that no one but me
noticed him. He sat down and read his
mail, and did n't join in the clatter about
the class races, because, knowing something about the subject, what the rest of
you fellows had to say probably did n't
interest him ; and he is n't a talkative
person, ever. Well, then you tried to
get him to subscribe to that foolish night
school for æsthetic butchers. I confess
his answer was not — not exactly urbane.
But it 's just possible that your request
was ill-timed."

  " Don't you think that 's one trouble
with Sears ? " piped the tiny one, who had
become interested. " He always gives
you the feeling that everything you say
is ' ill-timed ' ! "

  " The great, big, angry bull ! " added
Ellis. " And just the other day," he
went on, suddenly remembering another
of Wolcott's atrocities, " he took a letter
away from Billy Bemis, held him off
with one hand and began to read it, —
right out loud in the club ; and when Billy
snatched it away, Wolcott picked him up
and threw him clear across the room on
to the divan, and almost broke his back.

Now I don't think that any man who pretends to be a gentleman —"

"Oh, write a letter to the 'Crimson' about it —" yelled some one who, though trying to read in the next room, apparently could not help following the discussion.

"He was probaby feeling his oats a little that day," suggested Haydock, placidly. "Why should n't he? He's just like a fine stallion snorting around a ten-acre lot."

"Feeling his oats, yes, — that's all right," sniffed Ellis. "I suppose he was feeling his oats when he captained his class eleven, and used to curse the men out until everybody talked about it; that is, he cursed out the men who were smaller than himself — if it was n't worth his while to keep on the right side of them."

"For Heaven's sake shut up!" came from the other room, a trifle impatiently.

"Are n't we just a little harsh?" asked some one who had been listening without joining in.

"Don't repeat things like that about Sears, Johnny, even if you like to believe them," said Haydock, simply. Haydock always seemed a little older — less haphazard in his words — than his contemporaries, and never so much so as when repressing what had once been a temper of the most flaming kind. Ellis — limited, conscientious, uncompromising — created countless occasions for such repression. He was a pale tissue of all the virtues. His sobriety was the kind that drove men to the gutter; his chastity lowered temperatures. Once at a small dinner he inadvertently got drunk and became so austere that the fellows went home. To-night, in running down a member of the club at the club, he had more than irritated Haydock. And then — which in this instance was to the point — the member had been Wolcott. As a matter of fact, Haydock liked Wolcott as he liked very few people. But even if one was n't fond of The Magnificent One, he thought, there were so many people all over the college who spent a generous portion of their time in cursing him, — men to whom "Sears Wolcott" was the eponym of snob, and purse-proud arrogance, — that in not sticking up for him, or, at least, in not knowing what was really fine in him, one missed a rare chance of judging by standards other than those of Thomas, Richard, and Henry. Wolcott was a snob, of course; but then he never denied the fact, — he even volunteered the information at times. And there's hope for that kind of a snob, thought Haydock.

The club — which had a characteristic expression for almost every hour of the day — was beginning to lose what Haydock always thought of as its "just-after-dinner look." The men had finished their coffee; some of them strolled off to their rooms to grind; others hurried in town to the theatre; two were playing cards rather solemnly in a corner; on the divan, a worn-out athlete had fallen asleep over a comic paper. Haydock finished his cigar and went across to his room in Claverly.

At ten o'clock, — Wolcott's bedtime when in training, — Haydock lit a pipe and knocked on The Magnificent One's door at the other end of the long corridor. His coming at that hour was such a matter of course, that the door had been left hospitably unlatched as usual.

"How was the rowing to-day?" he asked. The question, also, was a matter of course.

" Damned hard work ! " Wolcott was
leisurely undressing and dropping his
clothes wherever he happened to be when
they came off.   " About ten racing starts,
then down to the Basin and up to the
Brighton abattoir and back.   I 'm tired."

" And just a dash peevish, I believe."
Haydock sat down on the floor, and lit
the shavings and kindling wood in the fire-
place.   Wolcott's rooms were always as
fresh and cold as the weather permitted.

" Oh, Ellis is such a God awful fool, —
I 'd break his face if he was bigger ! "
Wolcott looked at the fire a moment, and
thoughtfully stroked one of his bare arms.
" I got this, to-night."   He took a letter
from the mantelpiece and dropped it into
Haydock's lap.   Haydock read it while
The Magnificent One got into his pyjamas
before the fire.   The letter had nothing
whatever to do with Ellis.   Not that
Haydock supposed it had ; logical se-
quence in any two of Wolcott's remarks
always surprised him.   It was a tactfully
worded appeal from Barrows, the Recording Secretary, telling, with simple realism
that somehow or other stayed by one
after the letter was back in its envelope,

of a fine, keen, scholarly fellow in the
sophomore class who had been found,
literally starving, a stone's throw from
the College Yard.

" What do you think, Boy ? " asked
Wolcott, indifferently.

" I wonder who it is," mused Haydock.

The Secretary's omission of the man's
name had n't interested Wolcott in the
least.

" Why did n't he keep away, damn his
soul ? " he said.

" Well, he 's here, — that 's the main
thing."

" And Barrows wants me to give him a
yacht and some polo ponies, and keep him
in cigars and golf sticks."

Haydock made an inarticulate sound of
assent between puffs.   He knew perfectly
well that Wolcott wanted his advice,
that in his characteristic way he was asking it.   He also knew, for his liking was
an intelligent one, how to give it.

" Well, I call it pretty nervy," grumbled
Sears.

" Oh, yes — yes — it 's nervy."   One
simply had to agree with Wolcott in all
minor points in order to get anywhere.

"I don't like to have my leg pulled any more than anybody else does."

"No, I should n't think you would. But I imagine they 'd have difficulty if they tried to play any little games like that with you," Haydock added, confidently.

No one objects to being talked to this way by a slightly older person who is no fool himself.

"I 'd like to see them try!" growled the other.

"They know better."

"What do you call that, then?" Wolcott pointed with his toe to the letter in Haydock's lap.

"Oh — that!" Haydock's manner was most off-hand, "that 's merely the penalty of prominence and wealth.   It 's tiresome, of course, this having to come up to the scratch all your life.   You know — sometimes I 'm mighty glad I 'm not so powerful as you are — not in a position to do as much for people, because I think — of course you never can tell — but I think I 'd be the kind of person to try to do it every now and then."

"This sort of thing would be perfect fruit for you, would n't it?"

"I'm inclined to think the poor devil would stop starving for a while."

"How much would you give him, old Haystack, if you were n't such a dirty beggar yourself?" After absorbing a certain amount of Haydock's flattery, Wolcott always began to radiate a sort of bantering amiability.

"Who — I? Oh, I don't know! You can't very well send fifteen or twenty dollars, and let it go at that, I suppose; that's too easy. I'd fix up some scheme with the Secretary, — he knows all about that kind of thing, — and keep the creature going; pay on the instalment plan for thirty or forty years," he laughed, "you know, the way people do when they buy a piano or a set of Kipling — or any old thing."

This was about as far as Haydock dared to go. He often wondered how Wolcott could be induced to interest himself in something along the lines suggested by Barrows, the Secretary; it was the incalculable benefit such an interest would be to Wolcott that made him wish it; and he had, as often, given the problem up. For Wolcott took the initiative in nothing; he never had known the necessity that compels one to. The only effort he was ever called on to make was that of selection. It seemed as if everything in the world — the Secretary's letter included — came tumbling to crave approval at the boy's feet. And he approved of so little — least of all, of the people (Ellis was one of them) who butted their heads against the mighty wall of his prejudices. Haydock, who, perhaps, knew him better than any one did, was occasionally nimble enough to clamber over the barrier. When he failed, he consoled himself with the thought that, unlike Ellis and some others, his head was still intact. For, in an odd sort of way that suggested the congeniality of mind and matter, the two were excellent friends.

"Well, 'I must go to bed and get strong for dear old Harvard,'" announced Wolcott, abruptly. He had once read that sentence in a college story, and had quoted it, with intense amusement, every night since.

Haydock leaned against the doorway, while The Magnificent One slid into bed.

"Bed's a good place, is n't it?" said

Wolcott, cuddling his sunburnt face in the pillow. "Oh, Haystack, — I want to get up at seven, — leave a note on my boots as you go out."

"Have you found any one yet to tutor you in History 19?" asked Haydock, from the other room, where he was scribbling a notice for the janitor.

"Yes, I start in to-morrow."

"I did n't know anybody was tutoring in that course this year. Who did you get?"

"I don't know his name. Oh, yes, I do, too. He 's a freak named McGaw; wears a black cutaway coat with braid round the edge, and looks nervous. Good-night, old Haystack. Don't forget the lights."

Before Haydock made the room dark, he took the Secretary's letter from the mantelpiece, and put it on Wolcott's desk, where it could not very well be overlooked.

II

IF the primitive custom — in vogue, I believe, at certain colleges — of choosing by vote "the most popular man," "the most unpopular man," "the handsomest man," and so on, were numbered among Harvard traditions (thank Heaven, it is n't!), Wolcott would never have been elected to adorn the first of these distinctions. He would have had a large and enthusiastic backing for the second, and some scattering ballots for the third. Yet the material perquisites of popularity were his, for Wolcott presented the thought-compelling spectacle of a disliked person, to whom every social honour was paid with as much regularity as if he had come to Cambridge with a pocketful of promissory notes that called for them — to be drawn out and cashed when due. One never said of Wolcott, as is said of some fellows, "He *made* the first ten of the Dicky" — implying a certain amount of enterprise or discretion. The assertion that he *was* a first ten man required no implication ; it was enough, for it was so ordained. Now this fact is one of significance, — of greater significance than any one, not a Harvard man, is likely to attach to the sophomore society (and it is a wise Harvard child that knows the mother of its soul). But just why Wolcott — arrogant, combative, unresponsive — had been a first ten man, is for a treatise, not a story. It is sufficient to say that he was one, and that it never occurred to his numerous acquaintances to question his individual fitness for that honour, however much they lamented the system that gave it to him. Wolcott himself never questioned it. Only in the circumstance of his having been omitted from the chosen first, would the subject have seemed to him in any way markworthy. His attitude from babyhood towards anything worth having, that he did n't already possess, had been one of imminent proprietorship. Once when his nurse, holding him up to the window, had asked in the peculiarly imbecile way of nurses,

"Whose moon is that, Searsy?" Searsy
had replied, as one compelled to explain
the obvious, "That's Mr. Langdon Wolcott's moon." The gentleman referred to
was his father. This attitude Searsy had
practised through the nursery, and the
fitting school, until, by the time he went
to college, it was an exceedingly muscu-
lar, well-developed posture indeed. And
that's partly why he was called Wolcott
The Magnificent. The other reason provoked less difference of opinion; he really
was magnificent. Everybody who knew
about arms, and legs, and chests, and
things, agreed that he was. And as the
people who don't know about such things
always have a deep admiration — either
frank or sneaking — for them, Sears's
imperial subtitle was rarely disputed. As
early as the close of his freshman year,
the name spread to town. Girls with
opera-glasses used to sit at back dining-
room windows on the water-side of Beacon Street to see him row past with his
crew. They took the same tender interest in the way the April sun and wind
tanned his back, that a freshman takes
in colouring a meerschaum pipe. In years

gone by, Wolcott and these young ladies
had — in the good Boston fashion —
cemented their acquaintance with the mud
that pies are made of. But wonderful
things had happened since then ; a lot of
little girls, with piano legs and pigtails,
had put their skirts down and their hair
up ; a chunky, dictatorial boy had become
very magnificent.

Altogether, Sears was not the sort of
fellow over whose welfare one would
expect to find many people worrying.
There would seem to be but little cause
for anxiety about a man who knew how
to spend an enormous allowance sensibly,
— if selfishly, — who, on the whole, preferred to be in training most of the year
rather than out of it, who rarely fell below what he called a "gentleman's mark"
in any of his studies, and who, as a matter of course, was given every social
distinction in the power of the undergraduate world to bestow ; yet there were
several very intelligent human beings,
who, when they thought about Sears —
and they thought a good deal about him
every day — did not meditate so much on
what he had, as on what he so abundantly

lacked. They wished that things were
different. And Haydock used to say that
worrying was merely wishing two or three
times in succession that things were different. One of these persons was Sears's
eldest sister, another of them was Haydock.

Miss Wolcott was the sort of Boston
girl that dresses like a penwiper, and becomes absorbed in associated charities after
a second lugubrious season. In the patois
of her locality, she was called a "pill;" a
girl whom Harvard men carefully avoid
until it is rumoured that her family shortly
intends to "give something" in the pa-
ternal pill-box. Whereas, prior to her re-
nunciation, dozens of Harvard men had
been part of Miss Wolcott's responsibility, her concern was now centred upon
one, namely, her brother Sears. She and
Haydock, unknown to each other, had
found the same reason for wishing things
different. After making each other's acquaintance, they worried congenially in
chorus. In their opinion Sears was not
getting out of Harvard College the great-
est things Harvard College had to offer.
They did not expect him to see them,

— that would have been demanding too much; the undergraduate who sees them is an extremely occasional, precocious, and, as a rule, objectionable person. But they wished earnestly that the boy might, somehow or other, be put in the way of feeling them — of realising, even dimly, that the world to which he had lent himself for four years was something besides two small clubs, a fashionable dormitory, and a class crew. They wanted him to know, for instance, that the steady, commonplace stream that flowed to five o'clock dinners in Memorial Hall, the damp, throat-clearing, tired mobs that packed Lower Massachusetts on wet Monday afternoons and smelled, the indefinite hundreds that sat at dusk on the grass in front of Holworthy to hear the Glee Club sing, were as necessary, as real, as himself. They thought that such a conviction, or even such a suspicion, would make Sears a bigger and a better man. They believed — knowing, as they did, how inevitable was the general scheme of his future — that if the glimmer of these things did not dawn now, when the horizon that bounded them all ended with the college fence, it never would. And they were perfectly right.

"Searsy is really such a splendid fellow," Miss Wolcott would say to Haydock, with enthusiasm, "I want him to do something." Haydock, too, wanted him to do something. But they never got much beyond that, although they had many satisfactory discussions on the subject on Sunday afternoons, while Mrs. Wolcott and the younger sisters (who were n't failures) made tea and conversation for frock-coated youths in the next room. It was perplexing to know just where to begin with a person like Sears. Miss Wolcott laboured under a disadvantage; Sears was not the person to take suggestions from a failure. Haydock was more to the point. But he and Wolcott were of an age and a class; and it 's so easy to be a bore.

The Secretary's letter struck Haydock as one of the few distinctly opportune requests for money he had ever heard of. After he had put out Wolcott's lights, he walked up and down his own room, smoking his pipe and thinking it over. There were several possible outcomes to the little situation. An act of charity may be ignored, it may be performed with the enthusiasm with which one pays a bill for a suit of clothes long since worn out, or it may stir up a confusion of fine emotions that have lain quiescent in one, like the dregs of a comfortable bottle. The latter kind of charity is the sin-coverer. The chances were that Wolcott would never think of Barrows and his man again. It was just possible that he might send them a cheque for fifty dollars, and be unbearable for the next three days. But as for his being in any way stirred, awakened, made to know what he was doing, to wonder what he might do, Haydock felt, away down deep somewhere, that it was quite hopeless. And for that reason, the mind of man being so contrived, his thoughts dwelt that night, as they often did, on an apotheosised Wolcott, a Wolcott who justified himself, who did n't disappoint, a Wolcott whose sympathies and judgments were as broad as his shoulders, a Wolcott, in short, whose inside was brother to his outside.

When Sears got up the next morning, he "puttered among dishes in his bedroom," — a thing he usually detested, —

instead of going down to the tank for a
swim.   He had stopped his morning
plunge of late, because, since he had begun
to get up early, he almost always met Ellis
in the tank.   Ellis was an offensively clean
person ; he bathed with much unnecessary
splashing, and changed his shirt with a
flourish of trumpets.   His noisy ablutions
got on Wolcott's nerves.   To-day the
peacefulness of Sears's own room, and the
indescribable beauty of the College Yard,
— spring in Cambridge comes to the Yard
first, — as he walked to and from breakfast, combined to put him in one of his
best moods, — one which expressed itself
in a slow exuberance of spirits, a persistent,
obstinate bantering of everybody and
everything that, although far removed
from ill-humour, was not yet mirth.
When at nine o'clock there was a knock
on his door, Sears, instead of saying,
"Come in," called out the long, unspell-
able "Ay-y-y-y-y," one hears so many
times a day around college ; when he
looked up and saw McGaw, the tutor,
standing in the doorway, his manner did
not change.

"Hello ! — sorry to see you !" he said,

without rising. "I don't feel much like it this morning." McGaw fingered his note-book uneasily. "But come in, anyhow — I suppose I have to," added Wolcott, noticing with a smile that the tutor thought he had been dismissed. "Don't sit there; it's a rotten sofa. Sit over by the window and smoke."

"I don't smoke, thank you," said McGaw, sitting down where he had been told to.

"What's the matter; are you in training?" Let it be said, to Wolcott's credit, that the irony of his question was unconscious, and, to his discredit, that the chuckle with which he greeted his own words as soon as their absurdity dawned on him was pointed and uncontrolled. He had asked McGaw if he was in training, because the question naturally followed a refusal to drink or smoke; its inappropriateness flashed upon him afterwards. Nothing short of incongruity, striking, absolute, could make Sears laugh as he was laughing now. McGaw in training! That hatchet-faced, slant-shouldered, chestless, leggy, comic valentine whose neck and wrists and ankles

refused to desist where his clothes left off,
— in training! Sears twisted half-way
round that he might have a better look at
the tutor, and, throwing his legs over the
arm of his huge leather chair, he shook with
amusement.   Then a slow, disconcerting
wave of regret for what he had done crept
over him ; it made him warm, and pricked
painfully among the roots of his hair.   It
left him all at once with nothing to say.
McGaw opened his note-book and stared
at it blindly.   Two brilliant spots of pink
tipped his high cheek-bones.

" Let 's begin," said Wolcott, gruffly.

" How much do you know of the subject? " asked McGaw, in a voice that
might have come from an automaton.

" Nothing."

" Do you know any Latin ? "

" Damned little ! "

The tutor drummed thoughtfully with
his finger-tips on the note-book.

" Perhaps you 'd better get some writing
materials and take down the main head-
ings," he suggested.   " It 's an aid to the
memory."   He looked fixedly out of the
window into a mist of young green, while
Sears rummaged all over the room.   It

was some time before he could find paper
of any kind ; his desk was heavy with a
variety of silver-topped Christmas presents,
but lacking in any of the essentials for
study. He succeeded, finally, in produc-
ing from a drawer some undersized note-
paper, with the number of his room
stamped in blue at the top. McGaw
furnished the pencil. Then began a
travesty on education that was, no doubt,
being enacted in any number of rooms at
Harvard, at that identical hour. The
keen-faced, hectic-looking tutor, with his
exhaustive notes, nervously outlined a
period of the world's history, the importance of which both he and Wolcott
considered only in its relation to the
final examinations. Charlemagne's reign,
looked at as something of a stride in the
march of progress, would have bored
Sears and frittered away McGaw's time.
Had popes and kings been for an instant
regarded as more than names with a post-
script of Roman numerals and dates,
Wolcott's brain would have struck, and
the tutor's imagination would have creaked,
in the exercise of a disused function.
Queens, treaties, battles, diets, bulls,

crownings, and decapitations — for two
stifling hours, McGaw shovelled them
into Wolcott, until he sweat like a stoker.
And Sears, phlegmatic, colossal, consumed
them all like an ogre at his dinner.   From
time to time, he changed his seat and
began afresh ; it was as if he were setting
his teeth to keep the mess down until he
could disgorge it — the facts of five hundred years — on his blue book.   Only
once did he interrupt, and show, by asking a child's question about the unfortunate emperor forced to stand barefooted
in the snow all night, that any of these
facts were attached in his mind to human
beings.   Since he had come to Harvard,
Wolcott had done this sort of thing
before every midyear and final examination period.   He intended to keep on
doing it until, at the end of four years,
the President and Faculty would say to
him, in a communication that crackled
deliciously when its pink ribbons were
untied : — " *Sears* (or perhaps " *Sear-
olus*") *Wolcott, 2nd, alumnum ad gradum
Baccalaurei in Artibus admisimus, eique dedi-
mus et concessimus omnia insignia et jura ad
hunc honorem spectantia.*"

After two hours, McGaw closed his book, Sears dropped his notes and pencil on the floor, and leaned back with his arms above his head. The soft spring air, enervating with the smell of damp earth and new leaves, was finding its way up through the open windows. The tutor rubbed his strained eyes wearily; he had something more to say connected with the examination, but for the moment he could n't recall it.

"Oh, yes," he said abruptly; "we 'd better leave the Latin documents until the end. Most of them are translated in Van Witz's 'Mediæval Records.' I advise you to buy the volume and begin to look it over by yourself."

"I wish you 'd get it for me," Wolcott answered, after a moment in which he decided that the effort of picking up his pencil and paper and writing down the title was too great.

"I suppose I could," said McGaw, slowly. He knew very well that he could n't; he did n't have the necessary dollar.

"Yes, bring it round next time you come; there 's plenty of time," added Sears.

To almost any one else, McGaw would have had no difficulty in saying, " I wish you would get it yourself." But he shrank from what he imagined would be Wolcott's reception of such a request. For from the time he had come into the room, and found his big pupil sprawling unconcernedly in the middle of it, the tutor had been in a whirl of uneasiness and re-sentment. Wolcott's study was a very masculine, almost an austere apartment. But it was simple with the simplicity that costs a great deal of money. Its plain hard woods and dull green leather overpowered McGaw; the solid aggressiveness of Wol-cott himself angered him. Both the tutor's environment and his audience repelled an admission of poverty. In his embarrassment at having to say anything, he said it all, nervously blurting out:

" I 'm afraid you 'll have to get it your-self. It 's an expensive book; I can't afford it."

" Why, that's all right," said Sears, heartily; "what's the name of the thing?" He was as ill at ease as McGaw himself, now, and his abrupt note of sincerity was decidedly awkward. The tutor, of course,

immediately discovered the intent to pat-
ronise, that, as a matter of fact, was not
there. His hatred of Wolcott dated itself
from that instant.

After McGaw was well out of the
building, Sears would have strolled aimlessly down into the sunshine — he never
stayed in his room any more than was
necessary — had he not come across the
Secretary's letter when he went to his
desk to put away the notes he had just
taken. He reread this document, with
what is conveniently known as "mingled
emotions." That is to say, his impatience
at the Secretary's "nerve" diffused itself,
as he read, in a vague inclination to know
exactly what Barrows wanted him to do.
He would not for anything have acknowledged, even to himself, that his two hours
with McGaw had brought about this
frame of mind, which in Sears was
almost equivalent to mellowness. He
preferred to think that Haydock's opinions were worth respecting. But, nevertheless, it was McGaw with his pinched,
hectic, angular, hunted personality, all
sticking out of a scant, tightly-buttoned
cutaway coat, that had induced Sears, by

some curiously indirect mental process, to reread the letter in the first place. For, after all, Wolcott was a gentleman, if an extremely young one, and when he hurt people's feelings, as he very often did, he always felt uncomfortable about it after-wards. Not that his discomfort brought him to the point of an apology, — some day, perhaps, it might. But then, if he ever became softened to that extent he probably would n't offend any one in the first place. He read the Secretary's busi-ness-like statements about the man whose breakfasts and luncheons and dinners were oatmeal, oatmeal, and oatmeal, and a little milk — condensed milk. But it was McGaw himself who managed to put the breath of life into the written pages, and make the man they told about seem any more vital than Charlemagne or Martin Luther; words alone rarely told Wolcott much. McGaw's glowing cheek-bones, his drawn, sensitive mouth, and stringy clothes were pleading his own cause, unknown to himself, to Wolcott, or to the Secretary.

Sears put down the letter and drew a sheet of the little note-paper to him.

Then, after beating a preliminary tattoo, that sounded like the clicking of a telegraph instrument, with his pen, he wrote to Barrows : " I shall be glad to do what I can for your man ; but you must tell me what it is you want me to do. Can I see you some time and talk it over ? " On his way out to post the note, he met Haydock.

" I bet you 'd like to know what 's inside this, Haystack," he said, thrusting the envelope into his friend's face and chuckling inscrutably. Haydock looked at the address.

" You 'll tell me some day," he answered confidently. Wolcott jerked his note away. His reply was : —

" I 'll be damned if I do ! " He meant what he said at the time because he knew Haydock was interested and thought he could tease him. As a rule, he found it impossible to tease Haydock, unless he pulled his hair or knocked him down.

III

AFTER one has been out of college long enough to reckon time by a calendar, instead of by the college catalogue, May and June are sprightly preludes to all one's operas unsung. But when the year counts nine months, instead of twelve, spring is a climax. At Harvard, it comes in a misty veil of young elm leaves and apple blossoms that floats, for a time, with the sweetest deception in the world, between you and every other disagreeable fact. It envelops you, permeates you, seduces you, and makes you drunk; yet, as hour after hour (and lecture after lecture) drifts past your open window, or your canoe, or the sun-flecked lawn under the trees in the Yard, where you lie and watch the industrious robins rip elastic angle-worms from the sod, you believe that you have awakened for the first time, — that the problem has at last solved itself. You are as blind as a poet, and you laugh and wonder why you never saw before. Had not the only verse been written, you would write it: "Come . . . sit by my side and let the world slip; we shall ne'er be younger."

But in spite of all this, these first spring days, that incline one to look upon the immoral sense as a sort of hibernating beast, are not beginnings but the end. A feeling as of many things happening at once comes over you. There is much to do, and no time whatever in which to do it. The College is in a hurry. It crashes along toward the Finals and Class Day, carrying you with it in spite of you. No single activity in which you may engage seems in itself of utmost importance. But the sum total crowds your days and nights with the interests of rowing and base-ball, and the First Ten, and the perennial squabbles of the three clubs in their efforts to pledge the most attractive of the neophytes to join their respective institutions (which, unless the neophytes are very sensible young men, does n't tend to make them any more attractive), and the great Spring Dinners, when the graduates come back and meet all the new men and sing

songs and drink drinks (or is it the other
way?), and forget that they have ever been
away from Harvard at all, and the dinners
of the college papers, — "The Monthly"
(roistering blades), at some modest tavern;
and "The Advocate," at Marliave's, perhaps, with nothing in particular to eat, but
with all that easy indifference to the fra-
gility of crockery by which the artistic
temperament makes itself heard; "The
Crimson" (typographical remonstrance),
enjoying itself somewhere in its strange,
reproachful way; and the "Only Successful," "The Lampoon," at The Empire or
The Tuileries, laughing all night regardless
of expense.   Then there is Strawberry
Night at the Signet, when the First Seven,
from the Sophomore Class is taken in, —
Haydock and Ellis were on the First Seven,
— and the O. K. dinner (Hush-h-h-h-h!),
when the First Eight from the Junior
Class is initiated, and Strawberry Night at
the Pudding, and the "Pop" Concerts,
and Riverside, and a thousand other delightful happenings.   None of them are
of supreme importance, I suppose.   But
they combine to whirl certain men through
May and part of June on a strong, swift

current of Harvard life that deposits them, after Class Day and Commencement, somewhere high and dry and — although they may not know it themselves — homesick for Cambridge.

Even the mildest, farthest-meandering eddies of this current do not reach the type of student to which McGaw belonged ; McGaw knew nothing of them. He had not gone to college to drift with the stream. He was there, primarily, to acquire information along certain lines laid out in the curriculum, incidentally to fight hunger and cold and darkness. If he could be "sandy" and healthy and lucky enough to stick it out for four years, he would have, at the end, concealed somewhere about his person, that distinction (of many differences), — a college education. " Sand" he had, — an incredible amount of it. But the trait had bid fair to destroy his health before it discovered his luck. For to stay where he was at all, and slave with his mind, often obliged him first to exhaust and stultify himself with the manual labour of a lout. He had taken care of furnace fires, cleaned cellars and backyards, shovelled snow, and cut grass,

until these varied avocations, together
with the remarkable work he did in his
studies, and the farcical meals he cooked
himself, broke him down and sent him in
a semi-hysterical, wholly pitiful state to
the kindly Barrows. And Barrows, convinced that he did not belong to the many
"grinds," — of such admirable purpose
and tragic mediocrity, — who made the
Secretary's office one of constant anguish,
hit upon an inspiration. Of late, it had
seemed positively Heaven-sent. Wolcott
had come to him, and said, in a manner
that combined a child's shyness with the
omnipotence of a crowned head who believes in the divine right of kings, "I wish
you would tell me just what I 'm to do for
this man you wrote me about." Barrows
was gratified, amused, and, perhaps, a trifle
worried. His half hour with Sears, like a
good deal of the time spent in The Magnificent One's company, rather baffled the
Secretary. Wolcott's method of doing
charity was in itself extraordinary. Furthermore, as far as Barrows could see, —
and he was keen, — there was no particular
motive for the act. Compassion was lacking; what little Sears said was impersonal,

almost cold. Vanity, smug self-apprecia-
tion, there was none ; the fellow neither
enjoined theatrical conditions of secrecy,
nor showed ill-concealed eagerness to shine
his light before men. The personal equa-
tion was eliminated. Wolcott indicated
nothing but a princely willingness to undertake and carry out whatever the situation
required. As a matter of temporary con-
venience, he told Barrows he preferred
sending the man a monthly allowance,
to giving any particular sum at the
start.

"Tell him to spend his money and—
and eat things," was perhaps his most
specific suggestion.

Haydock, of course, was deeply interested in his quiet fashion. Sears told
him the bald facts in a casual, indifferent
way one afternoon when he was changing
his clothes to row. The interview with
the Secretary, Haydock was forced to reconstruct as best he could.

"Are you going to keep it up right
along ? " he asked, sceptically.

"Why not ? " Sears's tone implied the
usual chip on his shoulder.

"Well, it's very good of you," com-

mented the other, with almost imperceptible exaggeration.

"Oh, hell! — now you're giving me
the geehee; I can tell that even if I
can't write anonymous sonnets for the
'Monthly.'"   He gave Haydock one of
his athletic tributes of affection.   "You
know   there's nothing good about it.
What difference does it make?"

Yet in spite of Wolcott's characteristic
attitude to his indigent unknown, — it was
equivalent, briefly, to a shrug of the shoulders, — the two dropped into the habit
of talking together about him.   They
referred to him after a time as "It," or
"Crœsus,"   or   "The   Bloated   Bond-
holder;" and one of Wolcott's favourite
amusements was to describe in detail, with
an idiotic brilliancy of invention that Haydock had never given him credit for,
what "It" was doing at that particular
moment.

"'It' must be dressing for dinner,
don't you think?" Sears would ask, apropos of nothing at all.

"Oh, do you think so, — at six
o'clock?"   Haydock would take out his
watch, and deliberate seriously, "You see

he dines at eight, probably, and that gives
him just time to get away from the Somer-
set and take in the last few numbers at
the ' Pop ' Concert."

" Yes, — he won't care for long dinners
this warm weather," Sears would add;
" some clams, a clear soup, a bird,
a truffle or two, salad perhaps; all a
man really needs of course, but nothing
heavy or elaborate."

Or again: " ' It ' had better hurry up
and put that boat of his into commis-
sion if he wants to get to Poughkeepsie
for the race."

" Will he go round with her ? " Haydock would consider doubtfully.

" Oh, dear, no ; he 'll take his car and
meet her there. That sailing master of
his is a capital man, — perfectly invaluable
he's been to Crœsus. You remember
that spring on the Mediterranean ? "

" Oh, yes, yes, of course, that time ! "

After some such elaborate bit of fooling, Wolcott would roll on the floor in
paroxysms of mirth. And all the while
McGaw and Wolcott were spending several hours a week in the same room,
translating from the same page. Once

when Haydock tiptoed in during a seminar to borrow something, Sears glanced up from the Latin Documents and said :

"Crœsus has had a mighty pretty lot of ponies sent up from Virginia," and Haydock had answered, as he rummaged through the desk : —

" Good work, — I 'll have to look them over."

Long practice had perfected the technique of their little game ; its suggestion of mindless opulence was maddening to McGaw. He had very bitter feelings sometimes. Of late they had all come to an intense sort of focus upon Sears. For in him McGaw was able to detect every human attribute that he especially hated. Sears, on the other hand, though naturally inclined to regard the tutor as a serviceable, if unsightly, machine, became used to his high-strung, underfed personality. He would talk to him now and then, when the effort of concentration became impossible, ask his opinion of certain instructors and their courses, — whether this one was a "snap," and that one a " stinker," — what sort of frills he, McGaw, was going to get on his degree, and if he did n't think the college was " a good deal of a fake, anyhow?" This sort of thing was infinitely more galling to McGaw than a business relation, pure and simple. He remembered that, with other men who interrupted the study hour from time to time, Wolcott talked rowing or horses or — what was even more bewildering — nothing at all, but fooled and laughed with easy intimacy. He resented Sears's ponderous adaptability to his, the tutor's, own special topics.

While these two were seeing so much of each other on this uneven basis, May came and went, bringing with it the Class Races and all the other spring novelties. Wolcott's crew came in second in the race, with seven men in the boat. Some one had broken an oar, or a leg, or an out-rigger, — some one always does, — and jumped overboard. So the order in which the four crews splashed over the finish line was, as usual, a tremendous surprise to the black crowd that stretched along the Harvard Bridge, and the sea wall, and the stable roofs back of Beacon Street. Everybody — especially the girls — said the man who jumped was a great,

splendid fellow.   He was, of course ; but
the crews and the man himself laughed
a good deal when they heard it ; they
thought that the men who had to stay by
a disabled boat and be beaten by half a
length showed their sand.

One sweltering day in June, after the
examinations had begun, Haydock found
Sears in his room, staring helplessly at a
small mountain of clothing that reared
itself in chaos from his study floor.
" What 'll I do ? " he asked, mopping his
face dejectedly with the tail of a coloured
shirt.

" Why, what's the matter with them ? "
Haydock turned over a gay straw hat with
his foot.

" Oh, everything ! " answered Sears ; he
was warm and cross.   " They don't fit,
and they're hideous, and no good, and in
my way, and they make me sick."   He
gave the pile a kick that spread it the
length of the room.

" Why not let Crœsus have a whack
at them ? " suggested Haydock, thoughtfully.

" What ! " Wolcott looked quizzical,
astonished.   " Oh, that would never do,

Boy! It would be rotten for one college fellow to offer another one clothes."

"I don't see much difference between that and money."

"Well, there is a difference, just the same. The money comes through the Secretary, — a sort of reward offered, and no questions asked. Anyhow, there's something about money — something — Oh, you know what it is as well as I do! As soon as money belongs to you, it's just as good as anybody's."

"Rather better, I should say."

"Well, clothes are n't."

"Since you press me," said Haydock, fishing among a heap of crumpled linen, "I feel obliged to possess myself of this extremely pretty necktie." He smoothed a brilliant strip of crimson silk over his knee.

"Go on, Haystack, — what shall I do with them?"

"How many times does a simple statement have to be repeated to you before it penetrates?" Haydock rapidly began to bring a rough kind of order into the waste of shirts, neckties, odd gloves, and suits of clothes.

" Give them to Crœsus ?   That 's
out of the question, me boy ! "

Haydock worked hard a few moments
in silence.   Then he stood up, hot and
dishevelled, but amiable, as he always
was, and said, laughing : —

" That light grey suit, these shirts, those
neckties, and this hat, in fact the best of
this out-fit, is going this afternoon to
Barrows, with a note from you.   They
will subsequently be presented to ' It,
Crœsus, Esquire.' "   It amused Wolcott
every now and then to have Haydock
" boss " him.   The clothes went, of
course.

Two days later they returned.   That is
to say, the best of them did, — the grey
suit, the coloured shirt, the straw hat, and
one of the quieter neckties.   Ernest
McGaw, unspeakably jaunty, almost
handsome, was inside of them.

Even before Wolcott's bundle had enabled McGaw to blossom, like the season,
into fine raiment, his whole appearance
had undergone a subtle, indescribable
change.   Perhaps it was a recently acquired firmness of gait as he swung
through the Yard to a lecture, or up

the steps of Claverly to Sears's room. Hitherto he had hated the approach to Claverly; there usually were men going in or coming out, who looked at him as they passed. Once he had found a whole group of them seated on the steps, and had walked twice round the block, rather than brush through to the door. Or it may have been the spiritual radiance that comes of good food and plenty of it, money in your pocket, and peace in your mind. At any rate, McGaw's expression, whether it walked at you, or looked at you, or smiled at you, had, of late, become the outward and visible sign of a great inward happiness. Almost every minute of his day was dedicated to his work; yet he felt as if he were having for the first time leisure in which to breathe. By no means the least exquisite of his satisfactions was his first purchase of something unnecessary, a luxury, an extravagance; he bought one evening, in a dim musty corner of a Brattle Square bookstall, a second-hand copy of some Latin hymns for twenty cents. The demi-god who had caused such things to be — Barrows had spoken vaguely of "a friend" — had

become to McGaw the occasion of the
sun's rising and the stars' shining; through
him, the earth revolved, and the college
endured.   McGaw was very religious;
every night he prayed fervently for the
man who was befriending him.   To-day,
when he left his room to walk down to
Claverly, he had the uplifting glow of
self-respect and good-will to men whose
secret only barbers and tailors seem to
know.   Perhaps, just at first, he felt even
more like a white elephant than one
ordinarily does on getting into a fresh
suit of grey, after wearing black for many
months.   But the sensation, coming as
it did from the knowledge that he was
conspicuously better, rather than worse
dressed than most people, was not altogether an unpleasant one to McGaw.

Wolcott's back was turned when he
arrived.   This fact made what followed
even more unfortunate than it would have
been had the somewhat astounding truth
burst on Sears at the moment the tutor
came into the room.   For it enabled Wolcott to say, in his natural, off-hand tones,
without looking away from his desk:

"Is   that   you,   McGaw?   Just   sit

down and wait a minute." When his revolving chair finally did swing round, the transition was something very awful. Sears, in spite of his birth, and his bringing up, and his money, was, at times, to put it kindly, exceedingly " near to nature ; " just now he behaved as one might fancy a naked Zulu behaving were an electric car or a steam-roller to dart suddenly across his path in the depths of an African jungle. He jerked back as if somebody had made a lunge at him, and held on to the arms of his chair. Then he looked quickly from side to side, at the door and windows, with his mouth open stupidly. His eyes, round, rounder, helpless, turned again and again to that dapper butterfly in the chair opposite, who got redder and redder until all the blood in his body boiled through his face and away, leaving him white, rigid, terrible. And Sears could make no sound, only a gasping effort, until all at once the entire situation seemed to gather fresh force and smite him anew. He stumbled from his chair, through the door, down the long hall, down the stairs, laughing, shrieking, cursing like a maniac, out into the street.

IV

SEARS found Haydock studying at the club, and dragged him out of his chair, upstairs to a vacant room, and shut the door. Then he paced the floor like a caged lion, holding his hands to his head and exclaiming, whenever he could stop laughing long enough, that he had lost his mind. Every now and then, when words refused to come, he expressed himself by leaning against the wall, with his back to Haydock, and kicking the air behind him. Sometimes he pounded the door with his clenched fist. Haydock waited.

"I'll never get over this," Sears declared, "not if I live to be a hundred."

"Well, don't tell it backwards," objected Haydock; "begin at the beginning."

"There isn't any beginning," roared Sears; "it never began, I just looked around and found it there; it had been there all the time; you've seen it yourself." He sat on the floor and rocked to and fro.

"I'm almost inclined to believe that you *have* lost your mind," remarked Haydock.

"Just wait, just wait! You'll be a gibbering idiot yourself when I tell you, only you'll not believe me! You can't believe me! I don't believe it myself! Oh, if you'd only been there! — if you could have seen him! I was writing a letter at my desk when he came in, and told him to sit down. I didn't even notice him, or what he had on, or anything; and when I turned around — when I turned around — " Wolcott gasped — "when I turned around, I thought it would be McGaw!"

"Oh, go on, who was it?"

"It *was* McGaw! I'll never get over the shock of it." Haydock wrinkled his forehead at this clew.

"Can't you guess? Don't you know? Doesn't something tell you? Try, try! think of the only person in college he could be, if he weren't himself. Think

9

of the only way I could have found out,
the thing that made the difference —
the — "

" He is n't — he is n't ? " — Haydock
stuffed his fingers in his ears and shrieked.

" He is, he is ! " bellowed Sears.   Then
they both yelled, and made such a noise
that the fellows downstairs came running
up to see what was going on.

But they did n't tell them.   They
could n't, in the first place, and the fellows
would n't have understood if they had.
The McGaw-Crœsus episode was one of
those little interpolated experiences two
people own together so completely that
they can't share it if they want to.   This
one happened to be the kind over which
the partners could laugh.   When it happens the other way, — when two people get
together and cry, — it is n't nearly as valu-
able a factor in the divine accident of
friendship ; there is always one of them
who very selfishly does most of the crying.   For a time there was only mirth
over McGaw.   It was natural enough
that Wolcott should have but a one-sided
appreciation of the affair ; *he* had made a
discovery, *he* had been surprised, *he* had

found it very startling and absurd. It was not to be expected that he would stop laughing to consider McGaw's feelings in the matter. And Haydock, who was usually thoughtful and considerate, treated the revelation as he did at first, because it had come to him through Wolcott's eyes. Only when his interest in detail prompted him to ask questions, did he begin to reconstruct the scene in Wolcott's room, and feel intensely sorry for McGaw.

"What did you say when you turned around and first saw the clothes?" he asked Wolcott.

"Say? I did n't say anything, I just looked, and wondered if the exams had gone to my brain."

"Did n't he do anything?"

"Why, of course not; what did you suppose he 'd do? Tell me that he 'd changed his shirt? I could see that for myself; heaven knows I almost dropped dead!"

"Well, you certainly did n't just sit there staring at the man, did you?"

"Sit there? If I 'd sat there another second, I 'd have yelled in his face. I

crashed out of the room and exploded
in the hall. I came over here to find
you."

"Do you mean to say he's in your
room yet, waiting?"

"I'm sure I don't know, — I would n't
go back to look for gold and precious
stones."

"What do you suppose he thought?"

"Lord, I don't know, — I don't care
what he thought! What do you suppose
I thought?" Wolcott laughed.

"But if you ran out of your room that
way, and laughed in the hall, as you say
you did, he must have known you were
laughing at him," said Haydock, gravely.

"Why certainly he did! I don't suppose the creature thought I was throwing
a fit like that just for exercise. What
difference does it make anyhow?" Sears
went on indifferently. "I'll never see
him again. To-day's the last time he was
coming to tutor me, — 'the exam' is to-
morrow; I'll send him a cheque for
what I owe him, and there you are."

"But he must have thought you were
laughing at him because he was dressed
up," persisted Haydock.

" Well, damn it, I was ! If he had n't come looking as fine as a drunken shoe-maker in my old clothes, I never should have known ! " McGaw's emotions did n't contribute in any way to Wolcott's enjoy-ment of his discovery, — why should Haydock branch off and make such a tiresome point of them !

" It 's too bad you offended him that way," Haydock reflected ; " for of course he must be frightfully offended. He 's utterly in the dark about the thing, — he would n't have worn the clothes to your room if he were n't ; and he just thinks he looks like an overdressed fool in them. He 'll go home and take them off, and never wear them again."

" Then he certainly will be a fool," answered Wolcott, a trifle sulkily. " He looked extremely nice in them. If I 'd known how well they looked on, I should n't have given them away." He spoke as if he were perfectly insensitive to McGaw's probable anger and mortifi-cation ; but Haydock knew that he was n't.

" It 's funny, of course ; but I 'm mighty sorry it happened." The more Hay-dock thought of the way Sears had behaved, the more it worried him. "You can insult your friends without its making any particular difference, I suppose; they either refuse to take you seriously, or insult back, just as they please. But McGaw's different, — he's a defenceless, pathetic sort of a creature, and tremendously sensitive; I could see that whenever I met him in your room. He's the kind of fellow that makes you feel that 'something ought to be done about it.'"

"I think I have done a little," suggested Wolcott, embarrassed at referring to his own good works, yet desirous of defending himself.

"It doesn't put you in a better light with McGaw though; and his feelings aren't any the less hurt on that account. All he thinks is, that he made a ridiculous exhibition of himself in somebody else's clothes, and that you were coarse and heartless about it."

"I'm afraid you flatter me," muttered Wolcott.

"Come, now, Searsy, you know, just as well as I do, how people feel when you laugh at them."

The Magnificent One's laugh, when exerted upon certain temperaments, was indeed a terrifically effective engine. Wolcott's sense of ridicule was not fine; it was powerless to discover the one vulnerable spot and stab neatly. But if it couldn't dissect, it could crush like a boulder toppling from a precipice. "Remember poor little Bemis!" Wolcott coloured; he had once bet that he could make little Bemis cry inside of fifteen minutes, without touching him. That he had won the bet in eleven minutes and six seconds was a success of which he was not very proud. "This isn't as bad as that time," Haydock went on; "because you didn't do it on purpose."

"It was beastly, though, — wasn't it?" said Wolcott, slowly, after a moment. He got up and looked out of the window, while Haydock sat and smoked in silence. "Well, for heaven's sake, let's not talk about it any more," he said at length, turning around. "If you can think of anything that I ought to go and do about it, tell me, and I'll do it." He left the room, and, in a minute or two, Haydock heard the front door slam behind him.

"What to do?" thought Haydock.

The occasions that would have made his interference in the matter anything but an elaborate bit of patronising, were lacking.   Haydock never saw McGaw in the ordinary course of events.   To explain things, he would have had to seek him out, and begin in a way that would have sounded to the tutor like : " See here, my good man," — that of course would hardly do.   Besides, if amends were in order, Sears was the proper person to make them.   The conception of Sears apologising to McGaw was sublime ; Sears actually apologising, — Haydock imagined him setting his teeth, and blurting out the fewest possible words in which he could frame a perfunctory sentence of regret. That would n't do, either.   Haydock, usually full of resource when it came to rectifying other people's mistakes — he made very few himself — was quite at a loss in this instance.   He ended by telling himself that what he cared most about, after all, was that Wolcott should feel genuinely uncomfortable ; for the good of his soul he ought n't to be allowed to jeer at a man and then abandon him to his bitter reflections, without being talked to by some one. Wolcott had shown that he was "sorry," as plainly as he ever condescended to express that state of mind. The sensible course, perhaps, was to forget the rest as soon as possible. This Haydock attempted to do.

But it was far from easy. He and Wolcott went abroad together that year. Wolcott wanted to divide the summer between Dinard and Paris. Haydock had long wished to take a bicycle trip among a lot of Italian towns that, as Wolcott told him, no one but he "and another know-it-all who wrote a guide-book about them ever heard of before." They compromised on the Italian towns. All through the long vacation McGaw, and what Haydock believed to be the type he represented, intruded upon Haydock's meditations at the oddest hours and in the most unlikely places. For the first time he understood something a man had said to him the summer before : —

" Why on earth are you going to spend your vacation in central Siberia ? " Haydock had asked him.

" Because I want to find out what I really think about Harvard," the man

had answered, laughing. It was n't exactly necessary for Haydock to go to
Italy in order to think; but when, in
August, he found himself loafing with
Wolcott through a chain of dead little towns
that some one had strewn along the hills
and forgotten, he was able to discuss with
himself, — and occasionally with his companion, — as he never had been before,
more than one aspect of life in another
little town that, had he known it, is quite
as dead in August as any mediæval hamlet of the Apennines. The discussions
were intensely serious, unsatisfactory, and
in no way markworthy, except that they
concerned themselves with Ernest McGaw
in particular, and a background of shadowy
strugglers Haydock and Wolcott did n't
know much about, that they referred to
conveniently as "McGaws in general."
They were unable to dismiss the tutor
from their minds ; and when college opened
again, McGaw was dazed one fine morning in November on seeing his own name
on the first page of the "Crimson" among
six other names — some of them well
known — that, together with his, the
"Crimson" announced, composed the
Second Seven of the Signet.

It had been Wolcott's suggestion entirely. He was n't a Signet man himself; but Haydock was, "which is practically the same thing," as Wolcott said when he asked him to do what he could for McGaw. The plan of electing McGaw to the Signet had been such a simple matter for Haydock to carry out, that he could n't scare up a suspicion of the smug satisfaction he had always believed was the reward of having gone out of one's way to do some one a good turn. Even when Wolcott came to him with the " Crimson " in one hand, and patted him on the head with the other, saying : " You — are — a — good — boy," he did n't have any of the nice priggish sensations he had been looking forward to investigating.

"No, I 'm not," he said to Wolcott. " It was too easy."

" How did you manage it ? "

" There was n't much need of management," answered Haydock. " The First Seven is so dazzled by its own general brilliancy that it firmly believes that when it was elected, the list of really interesting men in the class was exhausted. So it goes in for proposing its personal friends

who are congenial, without being 'clever'
and 'literary;' and as nobody will vote
for anybody else's friends, they all get
tired of black-balling people after a while,
and compromise on some obscure and
very deserving person none of them
know at all. It was when everybody
was tired of fighting, that I bucked in
McGaw. I said he was a scholar, — he
must be if he 's able to make you pass examinations; and I said that we would
be keeping up the Signet's tradition of
electing representative men, if we got him
in ; and that the Faculty would like it ; and
that McGaw would give just the necessary
tone of seriousness to the Signet that I
feared we of the First Seven lacked. I
said that, because people are always tickled
to death to think they belong to something very serious, without being serious
themselves. It was the speech of my
life, I assure you. McGaw was elected,
on the second ballot, without a murmur."

"You 'll have to make him an honorary member, won't you? Can he pay his
initiation fee?" Wolcott asked, with elaborate innocence. Haydock answered by

unbuttoning Wolcott's coat and finding
ten dollars in his card-case.

" Now sit down and enclose it in a nice
little note to Barrows, so that Crœsus can
have the satisfaction of paying it himself."
He led Sears by the coat to a desk, and
dipped a pen in the ink.

" This highway robbery game is a perfect damned outrage !" said The Magnificent One, as he took the pen and began
to write.

McGaw was bewildered and charmed at
his election, for it is a great honour to belong to the Signet, although no one —
especially the twenty-one members of the
distinguished junior society — knows just
why.   He was also considerably upset by
his unexpected translation ; it demolished
an entire system of dreary philosophy that
he had built out of the struggles and bitterness of his freshman and sophomore
years.   He could n't, logically, go on
thinking himself an obscure outcast, shut
off from human interests, since he had
become so pleasantly conspicuous in the
public eye.   Some unseen, unknown
power had wished him well, and had done
much for him ; McGaw was happy, grate-

ful, and, at first, mystified.   But when the
extra ten dollars for his initiation fee came
through Barrows, he considered the mystery solved.   He prayed enthusiastically
that night — a great deal more than ten
dollars' worth — for the hallowed being
whose goodness was unfathomable.   He
also laid awake an hour thinking up a
suitable subject for his initiation " part."
Nothing that occurred to him seemed
deep enough for so intellectual an institution as the Signet.

On the evening the Second Seven was
initiated, Haydock — who developed an
oppressive sense of responsibility for
McGaw five or ten minutes before the
fellow stood up to read his part — felt
rather proud of him.   McGaw's turn
came between a humourous effort in feeble
rhyme, and a narrative that the writer
sought to disinfect, — when he became
aware that there were several instructors
among his audience, — by explaining apologetically, that it was " from the French."
McGaw's part was a dissertation on " The
Vocabulary of Æschylus."

" I was glad he did it," Haydock said
to Wolcott, when telling him about the

initiation later in the evening at the club;
"because I'd blathered so much about
his being serious and a scholar. Why it
was wonderful — monumental! Nobody
understood a word of it, after the first
page, and there were twenty-three pages.
I counted them; I had to look interested
in something. If there's a solitary iota
subscript in Athens this night that did n't
get ripped up the back and disembowelled,
I'd like to shake hands with it, and ask
it how it escaped. Professor Tenny went
over to him afterwards; they had a
lemonade orgy together and made Greek
puns. McGaw had the grey suit on;
he's really a rather fine-looking sort of a
chap; he does n't seem peaked and sticky
out at the sleeves the way he used to be.
All the fellows wooded up in great style;
I'd given Ellis a long talk to death be-
forehand, and told him the whole thing,"
— Wolcott made a face. "Oh, you don't
mind! Ellis is just the kind to think it
sort of nice and Godsome. In fact, Ellis
told me he was afraid he'd always misjudged you, and asked me what he'd
better do about it." They both laughed.
"It's funny," Haydock went on, "the

way fellows are willing to accept a man
here if only you can get the right people
to hustle around and say that he's 'somebody.' I was thinking that to-night.
Not one of those fellows had ever heard
of McGaw until I sprung him on them;
and Ellis went around telling everybody
he had 'a future before him,'—whatever
that means. Ellis is perfectly happy, you
know, when he can persuade himself that
some one he has just met has a future before him. He thought I had, for about
two weeks once. Well, what I began to
say was that, in a small way, McGaw is
right in the thick of things now. There's
no reason why those fellows shouldn't
like him; he seems really human in
spite of Æschylus; and if they do take
to him, he'll probably make the O. K.
and the Pudding, and wind up by being
Class Day Orator. When I left, he was
talking to that detestable snob, Baxford.
Heaven only knows what they found to
talk about; but Baxford was cackling his
mindless cackle. They seemed to have
plenty to say to each other; I didn't disturb them. Isn't it funny?"

It was "funny" to Haydock and Wol-

cott, although Wolcott, perhaps, wouldn't
have found it out by himself. When, a
short time afterwards, the Editor-in-chief
of the " Monthly " begged permission to
print " The Vocabulary of Æschylus,"
and the " Crimson " called it " a remarkably distinguished bit of research," and the
Signet remarked that real merit always
found its level, Haydock and Wolcott got
together and laughed, and were " just too
cynical for anything," as Ellis said, re-
provingly. They laughed, too, when they
met McGaw in the Yard or the Square,
— somehow he had become a more familiar
figure in the college scene, — and spoke
to him. McGaw always had a cordial
" hello " for Haydock alone. To Haydock and Wolcott together, he gave a
somewhat stiff nod. Wolcott, unaccom-
panied, he ignored.

" That young man will succeed," said
Wolcott, one morning after he had been
given — as he explained to Haydock —
" the frozen eye twice, in front of Foster's."

" Any one who can afford to make a
point of cutting you has succeeded,"
laughed Haydock. McGaw's indepen-

dence and "cheek" pleased them both exceedingly.

Haydock had some foundation for his remark. McGaw was prosperous ; he was happy ; to many of his classmates, he had become something of a personage. He followed " The Vocabulary of Æschylus " in the " Monthly " by " Life and the Classics," and " Hellas and the Athletic Question " in the " Advocate," — two intelligent essays that were happy in creating varied opinions among the readers of the college papers, and in causing his name to be added very soon to the list of the " Monthly's " editors. There are few institutions in college through which one's tether, so to speak, can be more indefinitely extended than through the Signet and the college press. McGaw's acquaintance became large and eclectic. It brought him work, — tutoring of all kinds, — more than he could undertake. It gave him an interest in college activities, and an intimate knowledge of them that enabled him to supply several Sunday newspapers with columns of unimportant but lucrative information and journalistic rigmarole. It made it possible for him at length to

return to Barrows one of the periodical
remittances and something additional, in
payment of what he preferred to consider
his debt. Barrows gave Wolcott, and
Wolcott gave Haydock, and Haydock
gave Wolcott's sister the note that went
with it. Between the lines they all read
the fine feeling that McGaw, with even
finer feeling, had delicately suggested.
McGaw was nearing the crest of the wave.
The grinds of the class, in discussing him,
conceded to him a dubious facility for
getting high marks in his studies, and a
somewhat frivolous knack of impressing
people favourably. But they agreed that,
at last analysis, he lacked the instincts of
a true scholar. The other men told one
another that he was "a terrible grind, but
a darned nice fellow!"—which was another
way of saying he was "really human, in
spite of Æschylus."

Haydock had taken the fellow's measure when he said that of him. The tutor
was thoroughly "human." He was inclined to like most of the men he had met
at the Signet in a frank, simple way that
demanded nothing, and ended by getting
much; with corresponding naturalness, he

liked being liked by them. Moreover,
the dreariness of his first two years left no
more permanent effect on him than the
horrors of a January passage leave on a
traveller who at length reaches port.
McGaw proved himself a normal young
person, by the comfortable manner in
which the general hopelessness of his past
situation receded from his memory, and
left behind it one or two sharp details of a
purely personal nature. He did n't, for
instance, recall very vividly how it felt to
go more or less hungry for several days at
a time; but, on the other hand, he could n't
pass Wolcott on the street without tingling
all over with anger and contempt. The
recollection of Wolcott's treatment of him
refused to soften and fade; the sound of
Wolcott's insolent laughter never grew
faint. McGaw still felt bitterly toward
Wolcott. The tutor was human enough;
and he had n't begun to show how human
he could be. He was something like the
little girl who, on being told that she had
big eyes, answered, "Well, if you think
they 're big now, you just ought to see me
open them really wide once." Whenever
McGaw came across Wolcott, he thought

of a remark a certain terrible old man used
to make to his enemies : —

"You.'ll all have a chance to get back
at me if you live long enough," this terrible old man was in the habit of saying
encouragingly. "The only trouble is,
so many of you seem to die at seventy."
McGaw often hoped that he would n't be
cut off at that age without having had
a slap of some kind at Wolcott. So,
although he did n't exactly seek an opportunity, he was by no means blind to it
when it presented itself, which it did with
gratifying despatch.

There was the usual delay that year in
electing the third and last seven of the
Signet. The first two sevens had met
three or four times, ostensibly for that
purpose ; but either there was n't a quo-
rum, or some one had always played the
piano, or read Kipling, or Maupassant,
or Catulle Mendes aloud, or given a lively
rendering of the dramas then playing at
the Bowdoin Square Theatre, or the
Grand Opera House, until no one felt
particularly business-like. It was pleasanter to drink beer, and smoke, and " listen to something," than to squabble over

seven men far into the night, until you began to yawn, and discovered that you did n't care whether they or any one else ever got into the Signet. As time went on, Ellis and Haviland, the president, made several attempts to impress upon the society what Ellis called, " the gravity of the situation." But almost every one knew the president too well to be in the least impressed, and Ellis's gravity was never very infectious ; so the Signet took its own time. When, at last, fourteen men turned up in the long, dingy room of the society one rainy night in May, and no one had brought anything to read, and the fellows who played the piano were disobliging, Haviland called them to order, at the earnest request of Ellis, secretary and treasurer, and declared that the first business to come before the meeting was the election of the Third Seven. Ellis looked conscious and aggrieved ; he had written several pages of minutes in rhyme, and wanted to read them.

"You look rather well behind that desk, Haviland," drawled a fellow named Baxford ; " but you make a rotten president. The first business is the reading of the minutes." Ellis smiled again.

"Not at all, not at all," answered Haviland, unabashed, glancing at the secretary's book; "I am only too well aware that Mr. Ellis has written a yard and a half of poetry for the occasion. I merely hesitated to classify so delightful a prospect under the head of business. If Mr. Ellis will give us the *pleasure*—"

"I move we adjourn," interrupted Haydock and Dickey Dawson and Bigelow and a tall man every one called Tommy, all rising at once.

"I'm going to get a cup of chocolate," announced some one else. "Ellis's poetry is always so sensual, I can't listen to it unless I quaff thick, sweet, 'lucent syrups tinct with' granulated sugar."

"Have the things come?" asked Haviland, abruptly dropping what he considered his parliamentary manner.

"Yes, and there's beer," answered Baxford, who was sitting where he could lift the faded red portière and look into the other room. The meeting, led by the president, stampeded, leaving Ellis pounding on the table, and endeavouring to

make himself heard above the uproar.
He was imploring them to "be serious
just for a few minutes."   Haydock stuck
his head between the curtains.

"That's what they call 'Harvard indifference,'" he said, and disappeared.

They wasted, according to Ellis, three-
quarters of an hour over beer and chocolate, and would n't have come to order
again at all, if he had n't begged them
separately to do so as a personal favour to
him.   Then they consumed almost as
long again in interrupting the reading of
the minutes, to criticise gravely Ellis's
versification, to discuss his "conception
of life," as based on his doggerel lines, and
to call attention, wherever poor Ellis had
indulged in anything that bordered on
"fine" writing, to what Tommy referred
to as, "Those subtle obscenities the author
has sought, with ghoulish depravity, to
disguise in the bombastic periods of a
Milton or an Alfred Austin."   They
moved that Ellis be "expelled from the
aristocracy of intellect, and sent to the
Annex, there to be kissed in the face until
dead," and refused to allow the meeting
to proceed until the motion had been put

and lost by a unanimous vote. Baxford created an inexpensive diversion by throwing a pack of cards into the air, turning up his coat-collar, and exclaiming, as they fell on his head : —

"B-r-r-r-r, how the storm rages without! Think, lads, of the poor sailors on such a night!" Dawson set fire to the portières, because, as he explained, Ellis had said something in his poem about a "lurid glare," and he wanted to see what they were like. The conflagration was put out with beer, and Ellis was fined three dollars for "perverting youth." McGaw enjoyed the noise and fooling as much as any one. He did n't quite know how to stir up that sort of thing himself; but he was no more anxious than the rest to get to the serious business of the meeting.

It was late when they finally began to nominate the Third Seven. There were in all sixteen names proposed. An informal vote was taken on them, — "a sort of preliminary canter," as Haviland said, "just to find out what the general feeling was." The ballots were playing-cards, cast in Ellis's hat (when, later in the evening,

its brim was torn off during a playful discussion, Ellis was fined another dollar for
the ensuing delay). Baxford's room-mate,
Anderson, was the first man voted on.

"Although he is n't just the sort of a
man who would be chosen for the first
two sevens," said Baxford, in his little
speech just before the hat was passed
around, "he's really a perfect corker.
He does n't 'do' anything in particular;
but I've known him a long time, and
he's the most amusing sort of a chap,
when he wants to be; and — and I think
he'd be a mighty good sort of a man to
have on."

Of the fourteen votes cast for Anderson, thirteen of them were black.

"As an indication of feeling," remarked
Tommy, "the informal ballot is easily a
success."

"Not quite 'in touch' with the Signet,
I'm afraid," said Baxford, good-naturedly.
Some one moved to drop all names getting six or more black balls, and this,
after the first round, decreased the number of candidates to nine. McGaw had
put up a man named Carver, one of the
editors of the "Monthly." The nomi-

nation was a discreet one, for Carver was neither obscure nor very well known. He was the kind of person they almost all dimly remembered having met at one time or another, in the rooms of fellows they liked. This is n't knowing much about a man; but, at least, it is n't knowing anything against him. Then McGaw's manner of indorsing him was distinctly good. He managed to give the impression of having honestly picked out Carver, not because he was Carver's friend, but because he thought the Signet was on the lookout for that kind of man. He seemed to wish, in a modest way, to please the Signet.

"I can't say that I 've known him very long, or well," said McGaw, thoughtfully (the others had made a point of having been more or less born and brought up with their candidates); "but since I 've been on the 'Monthly,' I 've seen something of him. He 's a pleasant sort of a fellow, and he writes pretty good stories every now and then; although I don't think he 's what you would call 'literary' exactly. He is n't very prominent; that might be an objection," he went on, unconscious of the implied flattery; "but I decided to put him up because I thought he seemed like a good man, and that some of you who know of him might like to consider him."

"I know him," spoke up Haydock, glad of a chance to help on McGaw's candidate. "I thought of him myself. He would fit in very well." Ellis, too, had a good word to say. Carver was then voted on.

"Fourteen red and no black," announced Haviland from the desk. The crowd clapped; and McGaw felt the little thrill born of an awakened sense of importance and power in the community.

It took an hour and a half to elect the next four men, — an hour and a half of eulogy, discussion, diplomacy, compromise, — although, as time went on, the increasing indifference of the majority of the fellows as to who got in tended to reduce the election here and there, among those who really cared, to the process of voting "for your man, if you 'll vote for mine." Not that the arrangement did away with animated electioneering in different corners of the room, and vehement arguments that might never have ended had not some weary outsider called attention to the fact that they had long since ceased to have any bearing on anything. But it gave a coercive publicity to pigheadedness in various quarters that made a Third Seven possible. At midnight, five men had been elected, two places remained unfilled, and the list of candidates numbered four. Then, by a curious revulsion of feeling no one sought to explain, three of the names that had hung on with a fair chance of success until that late hour, were unmercifully black-balled in rapid succession and thrown out. This left but one candidate — a man named Leonard — and two vacancies. The hat went around again bringing back to the desk, among twelve other cards, the ace of spades and the queen of clubs. Two black-balls, if persisted in, kept a man out of the Signet.

"Now we'll have to think up some one else. Oh, Lord!" yawned Haviland. "Leonard has had two black for hours; I think he's hopeless. Somebody suggest somebody else."

Ellis glanced at Haydock as much as to say, "Now's your time." He had been

doing that, off and on, all evening, until
Haydock at last refused to look in his
direction.   Haydock was on the point
of attempting something rather impossible, and he did n't propose to ruin his
chance of success at the outset, merely by
being ill-timed.   He had decided a week
before, — as soon as the postal cards
calling for an election were sent out, —
that he wanted Sears Wolcott on the
Signet.   His reasons for getting Sears
there were not obvious, and Haydock
appreciated the difficulties that lay in the
way of making them appear so, or of
giving any reasons at all other than that
he wanted him.   His best motives for
wishing to "buck" Sears in were hardly
formulated in his own mind; he could n't
very well undertake to make them clear
to others, even if they would have carried
with them any weight, — which they
would n't have.   He was influenced wholly
by the same feeling for Wolcott — a
mixture of admiration and fond disapproval — that had led him the year before to
do what he could to interest The Magnificent One in Barrows's unfortunate.   The
little experiment had done something for

Wolcott, — a good that perhaps only
Haydock and Wolcott's sister appreciated
as yet, but something that was, nevertheless, worth while. Wolcott's horizon had
given a little here and there; Wolcott
himself was somewhat less intolerant; he
had ceased noticeably, to Haydock at least,
to be actuated in everything he said and
did by a kind of American adaptation of
the ante-French Revolutionary opinion,
that human beings began with barons.
He was still a selfish high-handed youth,
— no one knew it better than Haydock.
But his friend found him neither as egoistic nor as arrogant as he had been;
and he drew his own inferences. As for
getting Wolcott into the Signet — Haydock wished to go on with what he had
begun. The junior society seemed made
to his hand. He not only looked forward
to throwing Wolcott and McGaw together
again, — on a basis of equality, this time,
— he wished to put Wolcott in the way of
having to see something of fellows who
had a variety of interests strikingly
different from his own, and who came
together now and then to talk and read
about them. Wolcott came in contact

with men of many tastes at his clubs ; but
the club ideal was, after all, the placid,
unimaginative ideal of fifteen or twenty
pleasant young men with plenty of money,
it was only too easy to live up to.   Haydock had no misguided veneration for the
Signet as a learned or even a very clever
institution ; an undergraduate literary society could hardly be one or the other.
He did appreciate, however, the curiously
diverse character of its components, and
the semi-serious intellectual friction that
went on there.   For the good of Wolcott
alone, he hoped to get him on the Third
Seven.   The attitude was quixotic, in-
asmuch as it was rather sentimental and
as absurd as only a thoroughly fine attitude can be.   Haydock had talked several
men into promising to vote for Wolcott,
should his name come up ; and Ellis, from
a variety of strange Christian motives, had
done the same.   Ellis had become enthusiastic over Wolcott since he had
learned of the McGaw affair ; whereas,
formerly, he had denounced him as a selfish beast, he now called him a " temperament."

    " Do propose somebody — anybody,"

repeated Haviland. " I 'm so sleepy!"
Two of the men had stretched themselves
on the sofas, with the request that they
be waked in time to vote.

" Let 's only have six on the Third
Seven ; it would be so quaint," suggested
Tommy.

" I think I 'd even vote for Baxford's
room-mate if he were put up again," said
Dickey Dawson.

'It was just this apparent willingness to
elect any one and get away, that Haydock
had been waiting for. He stood up.

" I can't think of any one who seems
exactly cut out for the Signet, any more
than the rest of you can," he said ; " but
I don't see why that ought to make so
much difference on the Third Seven.
Why not get on somebody like Tony
Wilson or Jack Linzee or Sears Wolcott,
— not necessarily any of those three, but
some one like that. They 're athletes,
you know, and people outside will think
we 're trying to be representative, — that
always sounds well, and, besides, they 're
all good fellows. Any one of those men
would be surprised and pleased to be
elected, I feel sure."

" Yes, — they did that last year," added
Ellis. " Martin was a Signet man, and he
used to go to all the meetings and everything, and he was nothing but an athloot.
People laughed at first, but they thought
it rather nice. I 'll vote for any of those
fellows."

" Well, I nominate Sears Wolcott,"
called some one from the sofa, — one of
the men who had pledged himself to Haydock. " I know him pretty well, and
should n't mind seeing him in."

" Buck him in, — buck him in ! " said
two or three others, impatiently.

" And whoever 's been black-balling
Leonard all evening, for Heaven's sake
don't next time," added Haviland.

Haydock was relieved that it had n't
been necessary for him to nominate Wolcott directly, and that there was but little
preliminary discussion of his fitness for
election. One or two men did attempt to
agitate his probable lack of sympathy with
everything the Signet stood for, but the
tendency to hurry the meeting along
prevailed. A vote was called for. Haydock involuntarily glanced at McGaw, for
he knew where the strongest opposition

would come from. But McGaw's face
was non-committal as to future intentions.
The hat went around. Haviland and
Ellis assorted the cards.

"Ten red and four black," announced
Haviland, with a groan. The result was
better than Haydock had expected. One
of those black votes he knew would never
be changed; but the other three might be
tired out, as he and Ellis had combined
to hold at bay every other candidate as
long as Wolcott was in the running.

"Now for another go at Leonard,"
said Haviland, wearily. "Just what he
had before, twelve red and two black," he
added when the hat came back to the
desk. "Who is doing it? Get up and
curse him out like a man; it's a shame,
when all but two are willing to have
him in." But no one got up and cursed.
Haydock and Ellis were the guilty ones,
and they had nothing against Leonard.
No one else was nominated; and Haydock
said a few words about Wolcott before
his name was voted on a second time.
His manner in saying them was the artistic bit of hypocrisy he felt the occasion
demanded. Willingness under the cir-

cumstances, rather than eagerness, was
what he sought to express. He knew
the value of his own conservative personality.

"Wolcott gets eleven red and three
black," announced Haviland; "one better
than last time." Another ballot on Leonard's name brought it no nearer election
than before. Haydock was quietly exultant. The election was slowly coming to
the point to which he had all along looked
forward to bringing it. The fellows who
had promised to vote for Wolcott — indifferent at first as to whether he got in
or not — were beginning now to "root"
for him vigorously. Incited solely by a
desire to have their own way, they tried
to find out who was black-balling him,
and made speeches urging his election
that Haydock would n't have dared to
make. Their eloquence succeeded by the
next ballot in reducing the number of
his black-balls to two. One of them, of
course, was McGaw's. The other, Haydock felt equally sure, had been put in
by Bigelow. Leonard had been Bigelow's
candidate from the first. Bigelow had n't
disguised his enthusiasm for him since he

had nominated him early in the evening; he had, in fact, declared good-naturedly that if the worst came to the worst, he would black-ball his own father in order to get Leonard in. Once when he did n't happen to have any black cards in his hand, he had asked some one to black-ball Wolcott for him. It was undoubtedly he, thought Haydock, who furnished the second black-ball, and continued to put one in every time a ballot was taken on Wolcott's name. There was no reason why Bigelow should n't withhold it on the next ballot, Haydock told himself, if he, Haydock, and Ellis showed themselves willing to vote for Leonard. This would elect Bigelow's candidate unanimously, and let Wolcott in with McGaw's one black. So just before Leonard's name was voted on again, Haydock went over to Bigelow and said frankly:

"Drop in a red card for Wolcott next time, and as far as Ellis and I are concerned, Leonard will be elected at once. We two have been keeping him out right along." Bigelow looked surprised, then laughed and nodded as if he understood such things, and in a moment Leonard, amid a murmur of relief from the crowd, was declared elected. Once more the hat was handed from man to man. They were electing Wolcott now, actually electing him, thought Haydock. He noticed that Bigelow voted with the seven of hearts, then he looked in McGaw's direction to see how the tutor would take the news of Wolcott's success when Haviland should announce it from the desk. It was very late, and the rickety old room had grown chilly in spite of the two blazing chandeliers. Three or four of the men had put on their coats and hats; the meeting seemed about to end.

"Wolcott gets twelve red and two black," said Haviland, hopelessly.

"What!" exclaimed Ellis. Haydock turned incredulously toward the desk; he felt as if some one had played him a sneaking trick. He went over to Bigelow, astonished and rather angry.

"You voted for Wolcott, did n't you?" he asked.

"Why, yes, of course I did," answered Bigelow, irritably. Now that his own candidate was safe, he was anxious to go home. "I've been voting for him ever since he was put up, except just the first round." Haydock swore. He had taken it for granted that Bigelow had been keeping Wolcott out when, as a matter of fact, it had been some one else, — some one who no doubt was in complete sympathy with McGaw. His jump at the conclusion struck him now as an incredibly dull proceeding.

"I'm sure I don't know what to do," Haviland was saying. "We simply must have a seventh man. I hate to have the thing drag over until 'next time,' when we're all here to-night. Nominate Tony Wilson, or Jack Linzee — somebody — anybody."

"I nominate Tony Wilson!" drawled Baxford, obediently. Haydock and Ellis ostentatiously gave the new candidate the only two black-balls he received. Haviland grasped the situation at once.

"I think we'll have to come to some sort of an understanding," he said. He was tired and annoyed, and so conscious of the fact that he forced himself to be extraordinarily polite. "Two of us apparently want Wolcott enough to cause a

deadlock, — which I suppose is perfectly
justifiable, — and two of us don't want him
at all.   Lots of things have been said in
his favour, and no one has said much of
anything against him.   I think it's only
fair for the two fellows who are keeping
us here so late to get up and give us
some idea of why they don't want him.
We can't very well throw his name out
as long as he has only two black.   If the
fellows who are keeping him out have a
really good reason, we ought to know it.
Such things, I'm sure, won't go beyond
this room."   There was a pause, while
Haviland looked inquiringly from face to
face.   Then McGaw stood up.   There
was just a trace of defiance in his general
bearing that vanished as soon as he saw
that every one had turned toward him
with interest.

   "I suppose I ought to have objected
to Sears Wolcott earlier in the evening,"
he said slowly.   He looked quietly, fixedly, at Haydock.   "I have met him in
a way that none of you could meet him.
I wish I didn't know that he was one
kind of a fellow with men who have
money and friends and everything, and

different with the other kind, — men who can't afford such things. I'm very sorry that I've seen him laugh at a man because he was poor and underfed and dressed in somebody else's clothes, — clothes that didn't fit him; because I can't forget it now, when I should like to. I can't think that he has a good heart. I don't want to meet him here." McGaw said this very slowly and regretfully; and when he sat down he stared at the floor. His little speech left every one wide-awake and uncomfortable, and so silent that the fellows could hear the rain slapping in gusts against the window-panes outside. His words in the mouth of — say Baxford or Dickey Dawson would have been laughed at. As it was, Tommy murmured audibly, "'Kind hearts are more than coronets,'" but the observation fell rather flat. McGaw had been painfully sincere. He had succeeded, beyond a doubt, in "getting his effect." Haydock knew that just that sort of thing said about Wolcott, by some one who was liked rather than otherwise, and who more or less represented "the extreme left," was peculiarly fatal. No one else in the room

would have talked in that way under any
circumstances, although there were several men who did n't object to hearing it
done so authoritatively. Wolcott, who
had seemed to be on the verge of slipping into the Signet a moment or two
before, was now given seven black-balls,
and dropped without comment. Tony
Wilson was elected with a feeble burst of
applause; Haydock and Ellis were putting on their overcoats when the hat went
around, and did n't vote.

Haviland turned out the lights, and the
men groped their way — holding on to
one another and striking matches from
time to time — down the two flights of
steep, dark stairs to the wet street.
No one spoke of the election on the
way down. Had anything been said it
would have had to do, undoubtedly, with
McGaw's speech ; and McGaw was there,
somewhere in the dark, with the rest of
them. Haviland walked with Ellis and
Haydock as far as the " Crimson " office,
— he hoped to get the names of the Third
Seven into the morning paper. But they
did n't talk of the election. Ellis was
boiling with righteous indignation ; Hay-

dock was wondering who had been McGaw's ally in black-balling Wolcott; and Haviland was too glad to have it over with, and be out in the fresh air, to think of the Signet. It was not until Haydock and Ellis threw some fresh wood on the fire at the club, and sank into two big leathern chairs, that they felt at liberty to discuss the matter freely.

"I suppose it was hopeless from the first," mused Haydock.

"It need n't have been, — that's what makes me furious," returned Ellis. "If McGaw only could have had an inkling of who he was keeping out —"

"Yes, I think he would have been the first to turn right around and work like a pup to get him in," agreed Haydock.

"I felt like jumping up and telling everything."

"How awful, — think of the scene!"

"Well, it would n't have been much more damnable than it was! Nobody knew where to look. There was just enough truth to what McGaw said — that and the way he got up and did it — it was n't as if anybody else had tried to —"

" The difference is that McGaw really
cared," broke in Haydock; "there was
feeling behind it.   It is n't given to many
of us to have real, sure-enough feelings
around here in college.   Nothing ever
seems to happen that makes enough difference one way or the other.   McGaw's
one of the kind that has them.   That's
how he got everyone to vote for Carver
the minute he put him up.   He just felt
all over that Carver was the right man for
the place, and somehow everybody believed
him.   He slaughtered poor Searsy by
the same method.   You see he's the
sort of fellow who is destined to be listened to by all kinds of people.   The
masses like guts, while the upper classes
prefer expression.   McGaw has the in-
tensity of a fanatic and the manners of a
gentleman; his armament is formidable.
I should n't be a bit surprised to hear
some day that he'd started an entirely
new and plausible religion, or written a
book that really proved something, or
reorganised the Supreme Court on a less
flippant basis.   The creature actually has
beliefs; he's rather astonishing.   I can't
blame him for giving it to Wolcott in the

neck, when he had such a good chance;
but I'm darned sorry he was inspired to
do it."

"I suppose you'll tell Sears all about
it," said Ellis.

"No, I sha'n't," answered Haydock,
after a moment. "You see, you never
can tell how he is going to take things —
so what's the use? The Signet's nothing
to him, and he might be ever so much
amused that McGaw could keep him out
of it. But then, again, it's quite likely
that he'd carry on and swear like a
trooper, and never do anything for
McGaw again. I know him better than
you do. If I ever do tell him, it'll be
some day just after he's won a bet, or
beaten me at golf, or taken a prize at
the horse show; not when he's cooped
up in his room with sore throat, the
way he is now, railing at the weather
and Cambridge and the college, and
everybody who makes a sound in the
hall near his door. I'm devoted to
Searsy, but I don't think I have many
illusions about him."

"Oh, I wish we could tell McGaw
about him! It might make McGaw feel

badly just at first; but I'd be so much
more comfortable. Could n't we — just
to be just?"

"Certainly not," yawned Haydock.
"One must have the courage to be
unjust."

And that, no doubt, would have been
the end of the McGaw-Wolcott episode,
if tailors did n't exert such extraordinary
influence over human affairs.

The next afternoon, when Haydock
dropped into Wolcott's room to see how
the sore throat was getting along, he found
Wolcott's mother and sister had driven
out from Boston on the same errand.
Haydock's call was opportune, for Wolcott, in a few minutes, had another visitor,
— a somewhat agitated, incoherent young
man who wished very much to speak to
Wolcott alone. The Magnificent One
would have granted the interview outside
in the hall had not Mrs. Wolcott protested on account of draughts, so he
took his guest into his bed-room, and
shut the door.

"How very mysterious!" said Miss
Wolcott. Her mother examined the

closed door through her glasses. "Who is he?"

"That's McGaw!" said Haydock, significantly.

"One of Sears's friends?" asked Mrs. Wolcott. Haydock laughed.

"I never knew that he was," he answered. Miss Wolcott seemed much interested; but her interest not nearly as eager as Haydock's. McGaw's visit baffled him. He couldn't believe that the fellow had come, in a fit of remorse, to apologise to Wolcott for having kept him out of the Signet, — the idea was fantastic — ridiculous. Nor could he think it probable that McGaw had found out what Wolcott had been doing for him; no one but Barrows and Ellis and Miss Wolcott and Haydock himself knew. The long interview in Wolcott's bed-room was indeed mysterious. It was something of a strain to Haydock to keep his attention from wandering to the rise and fall of voices on the other side of the door long enough to talk intelligently to Mrs. Wolcott; and when, after examining everything in the room, she said that, since she was in Cambridge, she thought she would improve the opportunity of making a call somewhere on Brattle Street, Haydock inwardly applauded the intention.

"He's not nearly as ill as his note led us to believe," said Mrs. Wolcott. "He wrote that he was 'wasted away to a shadow,' and that if we had a desire — from idle curiosity or any other motive — to see him alive, which he doubted, we'd better come out at once."

"I was reassured," added Miss Wolcott, "when I got a note by the next post, saying, 'Dear Josephine, If you wear that dowdy old felt hat, with the black satin bow and the brass buckle, out to Cambridge, please sit downstairs in the vestibule, while I talk to mamma.' Sears really ill is quite lamblike."

"So you see, you mustn't think me an unnatural parent for running away to leave a card on old Mrs. Burlap," said Wolcott's mother. Haydock saw her to the carriage, and went back to tell Miss Wolcott about the Signet meeting, and interest her still more in her brother's visitor. He softened the language of McGaw's speech a little, although he made its general import clear. His frequent talks with Miss Wolcott about Sears enabled him to.

"I agree with Mr. Ellis," she said, when Haydock had finished. "I want McGaw to know. It does seem unjust to poor Searsy."

"Maybe he does know," replied Haydock, listening intently to the voices in the bed-room. Suddenly they ceased. Wolcott burst into his loud laugh, and both men began to talk again at once. "I wish they 'd hurry up!" added Haydock, with suppressed excitement. Then the door opened, and McGaw, looking ill at ease, but smiling wanly, came out, followed by Wolcott, who went with him as far as the hall.

"And don't come before ten o'clock," Wolcott said, shaking hands. "I 'm not often in early in the evening." Wolcott, chuckling delightfully, came across the room, and laid a tiny oblong bit of white linen on Haydock's knee. On it was printed the name of a Boston tailor, followed in handwriting by Wolcott's name and a date and some cabalistic letters and numerals written in a clear round hand. Wolcott folded his arms and grinned.

12

Haydock knew where it must have come from, yet he looked puzzled.

"But I remember distinctly having ripped it out that afternoon before you sent them around to Barrows," he said, after a moment.

"Out of the coat,—not the trousers; they sew them under the right-hand pocket of the trousers sometimes,—so McGaw says," Wolcott laughed like a child. "That pressed the button, so to speak, and Barrows, confound him! did the rest."

"Well, well, well!" was all Haydock could say; he did n't like to let Sears know that he had told Miss Wolcott, and that she was eager for details.

"Who was that who just went out, Searsy?" asked Miss Wolcott, innocently.

"That? Oh — a friend of mine," answered The Magnificent One, winking at Haydock, as he took back the tailor's label, and put it in his card-case.

WELLINGTON

"IF I'd only known sooner that you were coming, I could have asked some of the fellows round to meet you," said Haydock, politely. No matter how well you may know a woman, you are always apprehensive when she comes to Cambridge that she has a thirst for tea.

"I think I like this better," his mother answered, stopping to look back. She was a lady of excellent taste, yet almost any one must have preferred the Yard that Sunday afternoon. The riotous new green of early spring had matured to an academic sombreness that made the elms, the stretches of sun-flecked grass, the tremulous ivy, and the simple brick buildings inseparable in one's thoughts. The dignity of the great space between Grays and Holworthy had grown with the late afternoon shadows, and Haydock and his mother, who had sauntered from path to path, listening to the leaves, and the robins, and the quiet confidences of the wise bricks, talked of Harvard. Although the place was large and deserted at this hour, it was far from lonely.

"Oh, yes, I like this much better," mused Mrs. Haydock again. Philip looked pleased.

"It's always beautiful," he said; "and there's so much else," he added rather obscurely. But his mother seemed to know, for she looked at him after a moment and answered, —

"I often wonder if all women can understand it, — the other things, not just the beauty, — or if it's only women with sons and brothers who come here."

"Especially sons," smiled Philip, taking her hand and swinging it to and fro, as they strolled back again toward Holworthy.

"But I never shall find out for sure," went on Mrs. Haydock; "because even the ones who do feel the place, just as if they had been here themselves, can't express it."

"It's so dreadful to try," said Philip. Then after a moment, "I was thinking of

all the horrible Class Poems and Odes
and Baccalaureate Sermons and ghastly
Memorial Day orators that are allowed to
go on."

"Oh, they probably don't do any harm,"
Mrs. Haydock interceded mildly.

"No, not positive harm," her son admitted; "but neither would a lot of hurdy-
gurdies in Appleton Chapel." Once in a
while Haydock was somewhat extreme.
Just now his mother took occasion to
remark on that fact.

"No, really, I don't think I am,"
Philip protested. "What can they add
to our feeling for Harvard with their trite
mouthings about *veritas* and Memorial
Hall? Other places may need that sort
of thing; this one does n't. Most of us
here recognise that fact, and conduct ourselves accordingly. And outsiders mis-
understand the attitude; Eleanor, for
example." Eleanor was a cousin with
Yale affinities. "I had to snub Eleanor
once for saying, before a lot of people,
that whenever she wanted to flatter a
Harvard man, she told him he was blasé,
and, if that did n't work, she called him a
cynic, and if even that would n't bring

him round, she hinted that he did n't believe in God."

"Eleanor is a very clever, silly little girl," laughed Mrs. Haydock.

"Eleanor is excessively cheap at times," corrected Philip. "We 're not 'cynical,' and we 're not 'blasé,' and whether or not we believe in God is nobody's business. If we don't drool about the things here we care for very much, it 's because people who do are indecent ; they bore us."

"They do bore one," assented Mrs. Haydock.

"Once in a while some one does tear out his heart and drip it around the stage in Sanders Theatre for the benefit of all the tiresome old women in Cambridge, and the Glee Club drones Latin hymns to a shiny upright piano hired for the occasion, while the orator calms himself with ice-water from the bedroom pitcher that is always prominent on those occasions. But such performances, thank God, are rare."

"Why do you go to them?" asked Mrs. Haydock.

"I don't," said Philip. "That was when I was a freshman, and did n't know

any better. Since then I have acquired
' Harvard indifference,' " he added, smiling
to himself. They left the Yard, lingering
a moment for another look down the
leafy vista, and walked slowly across to
Memorial.

The beautiful transept was dark at first,
after the sunlight outside. Then it lifted
straight and high from the cool dusk into
the quiet light of the stained windows.
Except for the faint echo of their footsteps
along the marble floor, the two moved
from tablet to tablet in silence. Somewhere near the south door they stopped,
and Philip said simply, —

" This one is Shaw's."

When they passed on and out, and sat
in the shade on the steps, Haydock's
mother wiped her eyes. The long, silent
roll-call always made her do that.

" It was a great, great price to pay," she
said at last.

" I never knew how great," said Philip,
" until I came here one day and tried to
live it all over, as if it were happening
now. Before then the war seemed fine,
and historic, and all that, but ever so
far away. It's been real since then. I

thought of how all the little groups of
fellows would talk about it in the Yard
between lectures, and read the morning
papers while the lectures were going on;
and how the instructors would hate to
have to tell them not to.   And I thought
what it would be like to have the men I
know — Alfred and Peter Bradley, and
Sears Wolcott and Douglas and Billy
and Pat, and all of them, getting restless
and excited, and sitting up all night at the
club, and then throwing down their books
and marching away to the front to be shot;
and how I would have to go along too,
because — well, you could n't stay at home
while they were being shot every day, and
thrown into trenches.   I don't think you
ever realise it very much until you think
about it that way."

"It seems, now, so terrible that they
had to go," Philip's mother broke in earnestly; "such a cruel stamping out of
youth and strength and happiness at the
very beginning."

"But it is n't as if you felt it were all a
hideous waste.   It did something great;
it's doing something now.   It can never
stop," Philip added, gently; "for every

year the new ones come, — the ones who
don't know yet. It's the fellows who die
here at college who always seem to me so
thrown away, so wasted," he went on.
"They don't seem to get their show,
somehow, — like Wellington, for instance."

"Did I meet Wellington?" asked Mrs.
Haydock, trying to attach a personality
to the name. She usually remembered
Philip's friends.

"Heavens, no!" answered Philip.
"Nobody knew Wellington, except a few
of us, — after he got pneumonia and died,
which he did last February. He was in
our class, and he must have been a nice
fellow; his mother was very nice. But
I'd never heard of him. It had just happened that way, — the way it does here."

"Where did you know his mother?"
asked Mrs. Haydock.

"Why, I thought I'd written you all
that. It must have been too long, or too
dreary, or something," said Philip.

"No, you never told me."

"Well, the first thing that I knew about
Hugh Wellington was that he came from
Chicago, or Cleveland, or some place;
that 'his pleasant disposition was appre-

ciated by all who knew him;' and that,
incidentally, he was dead. I read that in
the 'Crimson' one morning in bed, and
I knew exactly what it meant; because
when the 'Crimson' is reduced to the
'pleasant disposition' stage, there's a
good reason why."

Mrs. Haydock looked up inquiringly.

"I mean, they can't find out anything;
there's nothing to find out. He went his
way quietly, — decently, I suppose, —
without knowing any one in particular.
No one seemed to know him, not even
well enough to say that his disposition
wasn't pleasant; so the 'Crimson' gave
him the benefit of the doubt."

"It's the least it could do for any dead
man," said Mrs. Haydock.

"And the most that could be done for
poor Wellington, I suppose," added
Philip, thoughtfully. "After that, I
didn't think of him again — you don't,
you know; among so many it's bound to
happen pretty often — until somebody
asked who he was, at luncheon. There
were ten of us at the table, and Billy
Fields was the only one who knew anything about him. He said that he sat

next to a man named H. Wellington in
some big history course, and liked the
clothes he wore.   I think he and Billy
used to nod to each other in the Yard.
Well, in the natural course of events, that
would have been the end of him, as far as
I was concerned, if Nate Lawrence — he 's
the president of the class — had n't dashed
round to my room that afternoon to ask
me what he 'd better do.   Nate 's a bully
chap, — a great, big clean sort of a child
who breathes hard whenever he has to
think of anything.   He always wants to
do the proper thing by the class and the
college, and we help him out a good deal
with resolutions and committees and im-
promptu speeches for athlete dinners, and
all that.   He wanted me to sit right down
and help him draw up some resolutions of
sympathy and ' get it over with,' he said.
After that he could call a class meeting,
to which no one would come of course,
and send the thing home immediately.
I could n't see any particular necessity
for rushing the matter, except that Nate
had it very much on his mind.   It
was n't as if the man were alive and might
die at any moment.   So I told him he 'd

better wait awhile, and asked him if he
knew anything about Wellington in the
first place.   He said, why, yes, of course —
he remembered the name quite distinctly ;
Wellington had come out for the foot
ball in October, but had hurt his knee —
no, come to think of it, it might have
been his collar-bone — and had dropped
out pretty soon.   He was either the tall
lad with the shoulders, or that wiry little
man who might have made a good
quarter-back if he 'd stayed on.   You see,
Wellington must have been a mighty
quiet sort of fellow, because Nate is a tremendously conscientious president.   He
can tell almost everybody apart.

"I said, 'You simply have to get more
details, if you want me to write the letter.'
I 'm pretty good at that kind of thing,
but I like to have something to go by,
naturally ; it makes them easier — more
spontaneous.   Nate had been up to the
Office ; but I did n't find anything very
available in what he 'd got there, so we
looked up Wellington's address in the
Index, and went round to his room that
afternoon.   He lived in a little house on
Kirkland Street.

"It was a perfectly fiendish day; you've never been here in February, have you? Well, that's the time to see dear old Cambridge. It snows and rains most of the day, and then stops to rest and melt a little. There aren't any sidewalks to speak of — just dirt paths with curb-stones that keep the mud and stuff from running off into the street, so you have to walk in it up to your neck, if you want to get anywhere. That's what did Wellington up, I guess.

"The front door of his house was latched, and I was fumbling round under the crape trying to get hold of the bell, when the landlady appeared; you know — it makes me shudder now sometimes, when I think of that gruesome old buzzard of a woman. She was a typical Cambridge landlady, — one of those un-corsetted, iron grey slatterns who lives in a rancid atmosphere of hot soap-suds and never goes to bed; a room-renting old spider who manages to break everything you own, in a listless sort of way, and then writes home to your father that you haven't paid your bill. This one belonged to the class that looks on death as

a social opportunity. She was dressed
for the occasion, and greeted each of us
with a kind of a soiled smile that made
her old face look like a piece of dish-
rag."

"Philip dear."

"Well, it did. And then she said
in a loud, important whisper, —

"'He isn't upstairs; he's in my parlor,'
and took us in where poor Wellington
was. It was all so dreadful, that part of
it, that it didn't seem sad. There were
three other bleary old funeral coaches, —
more landladies, I suppose, — on a sofa
on one side, and a girl with fuzzy, yellow
hair, in a rocking-chair, on the other; she
was Mrs. Finley's daughter, I think. I've
seen her round the Square since. There
didn't seem to be much of anything for
us to do; and Nate was awfully embarrassed and uncomfortable, and seemed to
fill up most of the space in the horrid
plushy little room. But I didn't like to
go away exactly, because it made our coming there at all seem so useless; so I said
to Mrs. Finley,— I couldn't think of anything else, —

"'Have many of the fellows been in?'"

" ' No,' she whispered ; ' nobody 's been in but Mis' Taylor and Mis' Buckson and Mis' Myles. They come at two,' — it was then after five, — ' and the Regent. Mr. Wellington was a real quiet young man. He did n't have much company. He stayed in his room nights — mostly.' She stuck on ' mostly ' as a sort of afterthought, and repeated it ; the old fool had a passion for accuracy of a vague, unimportant kind that almost drove me crazy. I asked her if any one else roomed in the house. I knew he must have known them if there did ; no matter how objectionable people are at college, if they room near you, you can't help borrowing matches from them — I 've made lots of acquaintances borrowing matches. But no one lived there except two law students, ' real nice gentlemen, *real* nice,' they were, and they were n't there very much. Nate asked her when the funeral was to be, which was the most sensible thing he could have done ; for she took a telegram from her pocket, and said, —

" ' His mother 's coming to-night. She was in New York State when he passed away. They wa' n't able to get her till

this afternoon.'   Then Nate and I left
her, and I don't know why, — it was n't
idle curiosity, — but we went up to Wellington's rooms.

"They were bully rooms.   You can
tell a lot about a man from his room
here.   Wellington had no end of really
good things : rugs and books, — the
Edinburgh Stevenson, and that edition of
Balzac we have at home, — and ever so
many Braun photographs — not the every
day ones, but portraits and things that
you felt he'd picked up abroad, because
he happened to like them.   And on the
table — he had a corking big oak table
that filled up one end of the room — his
note-books and scratch block were lying
open, just the way he'd left them when
he stopped grinding for the exams.   And
there was a letter without a stamp, ad-
dressed to his mother, and a little picture
of his mother, with 'For Hugo' written
on the back.   Then I got to thinking of
his mother, and got her mixed up with
you somehow or other.   I don't know
just how it was, but you seemed to change
places ; I could n't see you apart for any
length of time, and I thought of you

arriving at the Park Square station all alone, and trying to get a cab in the wet, and having to pay the man anything he asked you, until I was almost crying, and told Nate that some one ought to be there to meet you — Mrs. Wellington, I mean. Nate agreed with me, and began to look panicky, because he knew I meant him. He really ought to have gone — it was his place. But I knew how he felt. He kept insisting that I could do the thing much better than he could; and it ended by my getting a carriage at about eight or nine o'clock, and splashing into town.

" There was a possibility, of course, that she would n't come alone, although she had been away from home, in New York, when she heard. But it never occurred to me that I could miss her if she did come alone, although I 'd never seen her, and felt sure she would n't have on black veils and things. You can't imagine all the different things I thought of to say to her while I was walking up and down the platform waiting for the train to come in. They all sounded so formal and sort of undertakery, that I knew I should n't say any of them when

the time came.   But I could n't think
of anything else — the one right one, I
mean.

"Well, she came on the first train she
possibly could have come on after sending
the telegram, and I knew her at once.
She was the very last person to get out
of the car.   It was n't that, or because she
looked different — anybody else would
have said she was very, very tired; but
I just knew her, and before I could think
of any of those other things, I took her
travelling-bag and said, —

"'I'm one of Hugh's friends.'

"I did n't see her when I said it, — only
her hands, — because I was looking down
at the bag."   Haydock paused a moment.

"I think it was the right thing, dear —
the only one," said his mother, softly.

"It 's a long, long drive to Cambridge,
even if you know where you are all the
time.   But with the windows all blurred,
and nothing to mark the way except the
rumble of the bridge or the car-tracks,
or some bright light you know pretty
well, that tells you you have n't gone
nearly so far as you thought you had,
it 's terrible.   We did n't say anything on

the way.   She leaned back in the corner ;
I think she was crying.   Mrs. Finley —
the landlady — heard us coming, and had
the door open when we got out; I made
her go upstairs with me, and told her not
to dare to go near that room and — and
disturb them.   She 's just the sort of a
woman who would.   It was almost midnight then, and I sat there until after two.
I tried to grind for a Fine Arts' examination out of one of Wellington's books —
he must have been taking the same course
— until the door downstairs opened and
closed, and I heard Mrs. Wellington come
slowly up the steps.   I put the book on
the mantelpiece ; it seemed heartless to
be reading there by his fire when she came
in.

    " She was a very brave woman, I think
— brave and civilised.   She walked slowly
round the room, sort of touching things
here and there ; and she stopped a long
time at the table, and put her hand on the
note-books gently, as if she were stroking
them, and then closed them."

    " Did she find the letter ? " asked Mrs.
Haydock.

    " No, I gave that to her later on — I

had it in my pocket then.   I did n't want
her to find it herself; it always makes
you jump so to see your own name written out, when you 're not looking for it.
Then she sat down in a chair near me
and stared at the fire.   I asked her if she
wanted me to go away ; and she said, no,
she was glad I was there.   We talked a
little — I could n't say much ; my position was queer you know — not what she
thought it was.   But it did n't seem wrong
as long as I stayed just because she wanted
me to, and I hated to spoil it by saying
things that could n't ring true.   She talked
about Hugh in such a quiet wonderful
way that every now and then I found myself wondering if she really knew.   Sometimes she doubted it herself, I think, for
she left me twice and went slowly downstairs as if she wanted to make sure.
When daylight came, she went in and lay
down on his bed.   I put out the lamps
and wrote a note saying where my room
was if she wanted to send for me.

"At breakfast I got hold of Bradley
and Sears Wolcott and Billy and four or
five other fellows, and told them they
simply had to go round there at noon,

and that some of them would have to go
into the station with me. They did n't
see any particular reason for it at first;
most of them were grinding for the exams,
and Sears had an engagement to play
court tennis and lunch at the B. A. A.
He said he did n't see why the man's
friends were n't enough without dragging
out a lot of heelers who 'd never heard of
him, let alone never having met him.
He was n't 'going to be any damned
hired crocodile!' he said. You see, they
could n't understand that if they did n't
go, there probably would n't be anybody
there but the preacher and Mrs. Finley,
and those horrible men with the black
satin ties and cotton gloves who carry you
in and out when there 's no one else round
to do it. But they all came at last —
even Sears, grumbling till he got inside
the gate. Nate brought three or four
fellows round from his club, and an armful of red and white roses 'from the class,'
he told Mrs. Wellington. It was a nice
little lie. I was surprised that Natey
thought of it. The Regent came, and
Mr. Barrows, the college secretary, and
poor old Miss Shedd, Wellington's wash-

woman. She was awfully cut up, poor
old thing, and made it as bad as possible
for everybody. That was about all, I
think.   Plummer, the college preacher,
was simple and manly; Heaven knows
he couldn't very well have been anything
else under the circumstances.   And then
we had that interminable drive again, back
to Boston.

"I was in the carriage with Mrs. Wellington. Any of us could have gone with
her just as well, I suppose, because we
were all Hugh's friends, although I was
the only one who knew that we were. But
I wanted to ride with her somehow, and
I'm glad now that I did, for a very queer
thing happened; I've never quite understood it. She did n't say anything for
ever so long, not until we got across the
bridge and the carriage began to go slower.
Then she put one of her hands on mine,
and said, —

"'I did n't know at first that you were
Haydock, not until I found your note.
I'm very, very glad to know, because
Hugh used to talk more about you in his
letters and when he was at home than he
did about any of the others. I think he

looked up to you most of all,' and she told me some of the things he had said and written."

Haydock often wondered if repeating things to your mother that you would n't repeat to any one else, made up for the things you could n't tell her at all. This passed through his mind now.

" I 'm afraid it 's just as well I never met Wellington," he added. " Well, there was n't much else. When we got to the station, I left Nate and the others to attend to things, and went into the car with Mrs. Wellington. She had the stateroom, — I 'd got that for her when I went in town in the morning, — and there was n't anything to do but give her her ticket, and say good-bye. I had a feeling as if I ought to go on with her and see the thing through ; but I 'd cut one examination already — I managed to flunk two more — and she probably would n't have let me anyhow. I did hunt up the conductor and give him the other ticket, — you have to have two, you know, — and told him to take care of it, and not let her see it ; it had a grisly word scribbled across it. She smiled when she said good-bye — oh, so sadly."

Haydock stood up and stretched himself.

" Did you ever hear from her again ? " asked Mrs. Haydock.

" Oh, yes, I had a letter very soon.   I had all his books and furniture and stuff packed up and sent home, you know. She told me to keep anything I wanted, because — oh, I 'll show you the letter some day.   I kept the picture with ' For Hugo ' written on the back.   It 's over in my room."   He went down the steps, Mrs. Haydock following.   They walked along the Delta, past John Harvard, and across to one of the paths in the Yard once more, sprinkled now with men hurrying to Memorial.

" It was such a queer waste, his having lived and come here at all," mused Philip. " I suppose that sounds awfully kiddish and tiresome to you, does n't it ? " he asked more lightly, looking at his mother.

" No," she answered ; " it sounded very old the way you said it."

BUTTERFLIES

JOHN RICE — somehow he was never called "Jack" — and Billy Ware roomed together, it was said, because their mothers were congenial. These ladies certainly had, in common, the bond of sweet stupidity, or they never would have put into practice the ideal arrangement of having their sons share the same apartment. Rice was always, and with justice, spoken of as "a very fine man." He was well put together and fine looking. His sense of duty was fine, also his sense of honour. He possessed a fine lot of commonplace ideas about many things, and carried with him an air of fine, if indefinite, purpose. On the whole, Billy considered him uninteresting.

Billy, on the other hand, was fatally gifted in his ability to please everybody. Other things being satisfactory, personal appearance does n't weigh heavily in the

balance of undergraduate judgment; it
was not Billy's extremely pretty and well
cared for exterior that compelled fellows
to take him into account in their preliminary survey of the Freshman Class; although that may have helped, just at first.
People who liked the plasticity of his
quick smile and the restlessness of his
black eyebrows — there was something
very un-Anglo-Saxon in their facial importance — thought he had "an expressive
face." But what it expressed, if anything,
no man undertook to say. Hemenway,
who drew for the "Lampoon," said it was
a sketch, not a face, — the sketch of a
painter who did n't take art seriously.
Neither was it cleverness that made fellows
who met Ware remember him favourably,
if they happened to be upper classmen,
and glad of a subsequent occasion that
threw them in his way, if they were his
own classmates. For Billy had none
of the talents of which parlour tricks are
made. In the presence of older boys, he
instinctively knew the number and kind
of remarks that gain for a freshman
the negative distinction of being "able to
talk enough." With his contemporaries,

he talked a great deal — almost up to the line that separated him from youths who chatter.   But except for a whimsical manner of attack, and his consistent frivolity of tone in regard to almost everything, his conversation was unimportant.   What he did possess, to a rather extraordinary degree, was that which, if given the field, is more magical among one's fellows at college than brains, manners, looks, or money, — that which is described only as " the indescribable something."

And Billy had the field.   S. Timothy's sent fifteen men to Harvard that year; he knew them all, of course, and roomed with the very fine one.   They all flocked together at first, until the acquaintance of each equalled the fourteen others plus fourteen times the friends of every one of them — which is all one knows, and all one needs to know.   The number — it included the nebular hypothesis of the next year's Institute and a few more — kept Billy's head wagging incessantly in and about Cambridge.   Of all this throng Billy was probably interested least in the man with whom he roomed.   John Rice was a constant and living reminder of

S. Timothy's; Billy detested S. Timothy's. He used to tell John pleasantly, that he not only did n't like the school or anything he had learned there, but that it had bored him extremely for six years, although he had n't perhaps realised it at the time.

"Spend next Sunday with you up at School?" he would say, airily, to this frequent suggestion of John's. "My dear fellow, how foolishness! My life-work consists just now in forgetting S. Timothy's." Then he would pull John's hair, or, perhaps, shy harmless missiles at him from across the room; for he knew that John was abjectly grateful for any semi-affectionate demonstrations of this nature, and it amused Billy to be liked by people, — people for whom he did n't particularly care. He did n't care much for John; he found him solicitous rather than sympathetic. John was too contemplative — too " set "; he refused to accept freshman standards and go ahead accordingly. Billy, who managed, before he was through, to spread himself uncommonly thin over a considerable area, fancied that he thought his room-mate pitifully prudent. For when Billy entered college, he proceeded from the very first to expand in the largeness and fulness of his glorious new life. People said, afterwards, his development had been so slight and so artificial, in the stained-glass atmosphere of his imitation English " fitting " school, that it made up for lost time at a most astonishing rate when the boy became his own master. He was very much like a supersensitive photograph plate in the hands of a bungler. If you know what *it* does on being plunged into the developing solution, you have an idea of Billy's Freshman year.

He had been such a nice little boy at S. Timothy's, — piping liquidly in an angelic " nighty " at Chapel, — that when the inevitable rumours reached there, the rector and the masters were deeply pained to learn that still another butterfly had burst from the godly chrysalis. They assumed lank, pre-Raphaelite expressions, and murmured, " Oh, Harvard — Harvard ! " Billy himself was not left in ignorance of their distress ; there was always John, of course ; and from time to time biblical excerpts, skilfully tortured into the form of letters, came to him through the mails. Somebody-or-other's pamphlet on "The Life Beautiful," and a horrid looking little thing in white celluloid covers, entitled "Daily Seeds for Daily Needs," were also slipped through his letter-slide one morning — all of which, in turn, caused Billy to murmur, "Oh, S. Timothy's — S. Timothy's!" His attitude toward S. Timothy's rapidly became that of one who places his thumb upon his nose and extends the fingers of his hand.

"'*Descensus averni facilis est,*'" John, in one of his more playful moods, had remarked to him one evening. To which Billy had replied, "Ah, yes — *E pluribus unum nux vomica facile princeps,* as dear old Virgil used to say." He was standing before the mirror in his bedroom adjusting an evening tie. Four crumpled failures already lay on the floor; from time to time Billy kicked at them as he moved about, or arrested the progress of his toilet to inhale deeply from the cigarette that had already burned several holes in the cover of his dressing-table. John was sitting on the bed, gravely watch-

ing the boy dress for the " Friday
Evening."

" Do you think you 'll come back to-
night ? " he asked.

"That's the delightful part of it all —
I don't know," answered Billy, with a
shrug. He had n't told John where he
was going after the dancing-class, because
John, by various pathetic little indirect
remarks, had displayed unmistakable interest in his movements. Billy withheld
the satisfaction it would have given his
room-mate to know all about him, partly
because he wished to discourage a growing
tendency, and for the reason that John's
— or any one's — serious concern always
aroused in him pleasant sensations of
silliness, accompanied by a desire to
giggle.

" After all — Boston is a busy little
place, is n't it Johnny ? " his smile was
radiant with mystery. " Don't sit up for
me, old man — unless you care for winter
sunrises," he added, imitating the tones
he so often heard in Sanborn's billiard
place, and laughing at the way they
sounded. " By the way, what are *you*
going to do to-night, — something devilish

of course, — but what ?" He was n't
asking for information; he knew that
John usually spent his evenings quietly at
home, or went to see one of the S.
Timothy's boys, and talk foot-ball or the
intricacies of English A.

"I ? Oh, I was thinking of going over
to Claverly to see Haydock," — Haydock
was a senior. "He asked us to drop in
often, you know," said John, so casually
that, after the manner of absolutely honest
persons who attempt a subtlety, he "gave
himself away."

"Translated, I suppose that means I
have n't been there very often — that I
have n't been there at all, in fact ?" said
Billy, sweetly. He was thinking to himself that when John aimed at "foxiness,"
he usually made a very successful cow of
himself.

"I may have been thinking that,"
admitted John, blushing a little; "but you
really have n't been there, you know, and
after the way you did n't turn up the night
he asked us to dine —"

"Turn up? Turn up?" said Billy,
with a giggle at an imagined picture of
himself turning up at the Victoria to dine

with Haydock and John. " Why, man, I
was dead to the world — I was a corpse!
Turn up? I turned up about two days
later, and did n't know where I was then.
If you had any gratitude in your withered
old gizzard, you 'd never stop thanking
me for not turning up."

" It was n't the right thing," was John's
comment. The appearance just then of
Dilly Bancroft, for whom Billy was waiting, averted the discussion — the one-
sided kind Rice and Ware always had —
in which Billy played matadore and pica-
dor, with grace and agility, to John's
brave but ineffectual bull.

" I 'm all ready. Let 's dash along;
you 're late, Dilly," said Billy, slipping into
his coat. He had a keen instinct in the
matter of personal antagonisms. He
always felt them long before they were expressed, often before they were even con-
ceived. John had never said much of
anything about Billy's friend Bancroft —
not even when that young man had seen fit
to break training some months before, on
the Freshman Eleven. But in spite of
John's hearty (suspiciously hearty, thought
Billy), " Hello, Dilford, how are you?"

14

Billy knew. Anything of the kind annoyed him — especially in his own room,
where he felt it his right to have whom he
pleased. He escaped with Bancroft as
soon as possible. John struck him just
then as a very tiresome person to be
saddled with. The two left, looking so
clean and well-bred and young and altogether inconsequent in their good clothes,
that John could not but smile to himself
and think kindly of them for a moment
as they clattered down the stairs and out
into the Yard.

Haydock was at home when Rice
knocked at his door in Claverly later in
the evening. It was always with a feeling
of satisfaction that one went into Haydock's study. Haydock himself had
none of the disconcerting habits of most
people. He never came to the door with
an open book in one hand and a green
shade over his eyes, protesting, with a
worried expression, that you had n't
stopped his work and spoiled his evening
generally. He never shook you by the
hand and seemed unnecessarily glad to see
you. He never began the conversation
by asking, after a stupid pause, the stupider

question, "Well, how are you getting
along?" It was impossible to feel that
your arrival interrupted him in the least,
as his door was usually unlatched, and he
rarely seemed to be engaged in anything
more urgent than filling his pipe, putting
a fresh log on the fire, or perhaps strolling
about looking at things, — occupations
suggesting somehow, that Haydock had
been trying to kill time until you should
drop in. To-night he was improving the
angle at which his various pictures hung.

"Do you suppose there ever was anything more maddening than a really conscientious 'goody'?" he said, as John
came in, — "the kind who has a passion for
dusting, a positive lust for it? Just look
at these pictures!" He straightened the
photograph of a Florentine saint, whose
asceticism, at a rakish deflection from the
perpendicular, had ceased to impress.

"I don't think we're bothered very
much by conscientious 'goodies' over in
Matthews," answered John; "one of them
broke Billy's pipe this morning."

"Has William taken up smoking?"
laughed Haydock.

"Well, rather."

"Surprising, is n't it," mused the other. He really was n't surprised a bit. He and Billy had been born and brought up next door to each other ; he knew the type and the temperament. He also was aware that Billy was an enthusiastic member of the Polo Club.

Haydock had tried to see something of the child during his first month or two in college.

"An older boy can do so much for a younger one, Philip," Mrs. Ware had said to him, with her hazy maternal trustfulness, just before college opened. "William is fond of you, I know ; and it 's a great comfort to feel that you will be there, and that he 's going to room with John." If the good woman derived tranquillity of mind from the fact that her son and Haydock chanced to inhabit the same town, Haydock did not consider it worth while to explain that the coincidence, regarded in the light of its moral significance, was unimportant. He had called on Billy and John as soon as they were settled ; but Billy had never returned the compliment, although John did frequently. Once he had asked the room-mates to dinner ; Billy,

he learned later, had been too drunk that
evening to recall the engagement for the
moment. Since then, the helpful influence, in the belief of which Mrs. Ware
existed placidly, had perforce exerted itself
across a theatre, or from the platform of a
passing electric car.

"Oh, I don't mind his smoking," said
John, with the faintest emphasis on the
last word.

"No?" Haydock kept his back turned,
and continued to touch delicately, here and
there, the corners of his picture frames.
As a matter of fact, he made some of them
rather more crooked than they were at
first. But he felt that if he did n't deter
John by turning suddenly and giving him
all attention, he would hear the whole
story; John very evidently had brought
one with him.

"Of course, I don't smoke, myself,"
John went on slowly; "it's just happened
that way, I suppose. But I don't mind
it in Billy. You can always stop if it
begins to hurt you. I think I like to
see him do it," he ended, with unusual
tolerance.

"Yes," agreed Haydock, deliberately,

"if it hurts you, you can always stop smoking." He, too, emphasised the last word softly, in a way that left the tale still untold. Haydock was something of an artist in assisting confidences where the spirit was willing and the vocabulary weak.

"Ware is really a bully chap; he was a perfect corker at school." John's remark was a circuitous paraphrase of, "Isn't it too bad!"

"He certainly is most attractive; I've rarely known anybody who was more so," Haydock assented, with an enthusiasm he genuinely felt; "but I don't see much of him now." His regret, too, was real.

"That's it! that's just it!" John burst out so hotly that the senior, who was filling his pipe at the table, almost looked up in ill-timed surprise. "Nobody sees anything of him any more; nobody who ought to, like you."

"And you," added Haydock, to himself. The situation was perennial; he divined it perfectly.

"Nobody but that damned Dilford Bancroft and that gang," continued John.

" Billy could know any one in the class that 's worth knowing ; he really does know every one. But you understand what I mean, they 're not his friends ; he does n't go to their rooms, and they don't come to ours. It 's always Bancroft and just a few sports like that."

" Cheap sports ? " Haydock questioned. He knew no more of Bancroft than that he was a decorative young person whose somewhat liberal views on the subject of training for a foot-ball eleven had stirred a ripple of indignation throughout the college in the autumn, and provoked some caustic reflections in the editorial columns of the " Harvard Crimson."

" No, I don't suppose they 're ' cheap ' sports," admitted the honest John, — " not the way you mean."

" Expensive sports, then ? "

" Well, if you mean that they seem to know how to do the things that ought n't to be done at all, the way they ought to be done, if you do them —" began John, a trifle obscurely.

" Yes, that 's precisely what I mean."

" Then they are ' expensive ' sports, I suppose."

"And Billy has become absorbed by them?"

"He does n't care to see any one else, as far as I know."

"Perhaps it 's merely a passing phase."

"I can't see that that cuts any particular ice, if he is going to be ruined before it passes," John objected.

"But he won't be," put in Haydock, confidently.

"What can possibly save him?" John was terribly in earnest. "His best friends are loafers and snobs; they never learn anything, and they all drink too much. All they want is a good time, — the wrong kind of a good time. Who is going to make him take a brace? I 've tried, and I can't; the college does n't seem to give a —"

"Hold on — hold on — hold on," broke in Haydock; "give the college a show. What do you expect the college to do anyhow? Supply wet-nurses for all the silly little boys who make themselves sick on cocktails at the Adams House?"

"It could do something."

"Yes, and does n't it, — the very finest thing in the world! Does n't it allow all sorts of men to come here, and give them the chance of their lives to learn about everybody and everything that was ever good or great or worth learning about? Is n't it willing to share the very best of what it has, — and it has everything, — its traditions and its knowledge and its beauty? Does n't it want to make the fellows here part of it all, if they only have the guts to keep their heads up, and follow along the road it has built for them? Is there any place else where you can live for four years — the four important ones — and know that the standard of everything held up to you can't change, like the trivial little standards of other places, that the aim won't swerve, no matter what happens, and that they are the highest, the best? Is n't that doing something — everything?"

Haydock was occasionally enthusiastic in a calm, thoughtful sort of way.

"I know what you mean — I 've thought about it myself; but Billy is going to hell. What about Billy?" John insisted.

"Oh, as for that — to pass from the sublime to Billy — he simply won't; that is to say, he won't here, at Harvard."

There was a gleam of hope in John's eyes. "Why?" he asked.

"Because he'll get kicked out," said Haydock.

"Fire Billy?" John looked terrified.

"That's what they'll do. And why not?" the senior went on heartlessly. "From what you say, he doesn't seem to be quite ready for the place, as yet; so put him out."

"But he isn't bad, really bad."

"No, certainly not; merely a damn fool; when he gets over being one, let him come back. The college understands that sort of thing much better than you or I do. It's not only highly intelligent, but extremely benevolent. I'm sorry about Billy."

"Won't you talk to him — warn him in some way; he'll listen to you," said John, earnestly.

"I should be charmed," answered the other, although he appreciated the delicacy of the situation, and felt that his words would fall on deaf ears.

It was later than John's accustomed hour for going to bed, when he left Haydock's room that night. This was his only reason for hurrying over to Matthews, as he did, when he finally said good-night to the senior. At the end of the little corridor near John's door a man who looked like a messenger of some kind stood peering out of the window at the lights in the Square. He must have been standing there a long time, — long enough to become convinced that the continual sound of footsteps in the entry did not necessarily announce the person for whom he was waiting, — for he turned to John only when he heard the jingle of his keys.

"Rice?" he drawled, "J. D. Rice?" He gave John a note, and sauntered back to the window. The communication was from Billy. John read it there in the corridor under the gas jet : —

DEAR JOHNNY, — Please, as quickly as possible, procure all the money you can lay your hands on — two hundred dollars at the very least — and come bail me out. I have been arrested and compelled to languish among hostile strangers. The man with this note will guide you to the scene of my incarceration. Please hurry, because I wish to go home.

BILLY.

P. S.   For Heaven's sake get a move on.

For a moment this document conveyed but little to John. He was obliged to read it a second time, and even then he stared appealingly at the messenger, who had turned and was eyeing him with feeble interest.

"They got pinched, did n't they?" said the man, sadly.

"But what did he do? What's happened?" John demanded. He was dazed; nothing he had ever seen or done in his life had prepared him for this.

"Why, they got run in," explained the man.

"Here — you wait for me here." The only thing John could think of just then was Haydock. "Or no — come into my room;" he unlocked the door and turned up the gas. "Be sure to wait," he commanded, as he rushed out.

Claverly was locked for the night; John remembered this after rattling in vain at the three doors. Then he called under Haydock's window. The senior answered from the square of yellow light above. He was on the point of going out anyhow, he said, and would join John below.

"Billy's arrested! he's in jail! What'll

I do?" John gasped breathlessly. He thrust the note at Haydock. "Read it."

Haydock struck a match in the shelter of a bay window and read.

"Why, the only thing to do is to bail him out," he laughed. "It's horrid, not to say disgusting, to have to stay all night in a jail. How much money have you?"

"I don't know, five dollars, I think," answered John. The darkness covered his astonishment at Haydock's calmness under the circumstances.

"I have thirty or forty myself, and I'll evolve the rest somewhere."

"Do you think you can?" To John the idea was incredible.

"Oh, heavens yes! That's the trouble with Cambridge; you can always borrow any amount at any hour. It makes every place else seem sordid and worldly. Is the 'guide' in your room? I'll meet you there in twenty minutes." He strolled away whistling. John hurried back to Matthews faster than before.

For ever so long that night was a hideous memory to Billy's room-mate. He and Haydock and the man — a sad, silent person whom Haydock courteously tried to engage in conversation from time to time — spent hours in chilly suburban street-cars and bleak waiting stations. Haydock ignored the topic that to John was of such overwhelming and painful interest; it was as if he had disposed of the entire subject earlier in the evening when he had uttered his prophecy: "Because he'll get kicked out." Grey January dawn streaked the sky when the trio, after finding Billy and Dilford Bancroft chatting pleasantly with the watchmen in the police station, managed to rout up the gentleman whose function it seemed to be to determine the amount of a criminal's bail, — he lived several miles away, — get a cab, and jog back to Cambridge. Billy talked most of the way, in spite of the silence with which John received his reflections, and Haydock's polite but unenthusiastic attention. Dilford covered his head with the lap-robe at intervals, and had hysterics; but no one noticed him at all, except Billy, who occasionally joined him in these complex emotions.

"It was the surprise — the awful surprise of it that killed me dead," Billy would giggle. "I was on the box-seat

driving, you know, — lickety-split, to beat
the band, with Harry Hollis beside me,
— he fell off when we went over the car
tracks. I'd like to know if he was hurt;
anyhow, the car did n't run over him, because I looked back and it never stopped.
Had Jimmy fallen out then?" he appealed
to Dilford, whose reply was smothered at
its birth. "Then we raced the car until
the horses — oh, they were corkers! — began to run away. I could n't hold them.
I tried, upon my soul, I tried! but I was
laughing so that my wrists were all sort
of tickly on the inside, — you know how
they do, — and I could n't close my fingers very tight over the reins; they just
flapped around in the breeze any old way.
So when the policeman ran out and yelled
and waved, what on earth could I do?
What *could* I do? We simply crashed
past him like a chariot race. I looked
back again and could n't even see the
creature — only Dilly on the floor, white
as a sheet, holding on with everything
he had. Oh, it was terrible! perfectly terrible! I was glad we'd bitched
the policeman, though; only we did n't!
That was the surprise. My dear, *what*

do you suppose that man — that devil — did? He telephoned — *telephoned* — to the next police station, and when we got there they received us. Policemen? There were platoons of them, — as far as the eye could reach in every direction. And they had fish-nets and lassoes and the most fearful-looking clubs; and one of the horses fell down, and everybody sat on the poor thing's head, — people always rush and do that when a horse falls down. I wonder why?"

No one ventured a theory, and William continued : —

"Well, they took us inside, and asked the most intimate impertinent kind of questions. I gave my own name, but Dilly did n't; he had one all ready that went with the initials on his underclothes, so it would n't be a give-away even if they had the nerve to go too far. What was it, Dilly? I've forgotten. He asked me what my occupation was, and I did n't exactly like to tell him I was a student."

"Of course not," assented Haydock, drily.

"So I merely said '*rentier.*'"

Haydock groaned softly in his corner.

" He just looked at me, — the great big thing ! I don't think he'd ever been abroad. Oh, and before I forget it, we have to be in court at nine o'clock. Now don't go and oversleep yourself, John, the way you do sometimes ; because I must get up whether I want to or not, I suppose. Where was I ? Oh, yes ; after he'd asked all the questions he could think of, I wrote the note, and we waited a deuce of a while. But it wasn't so bad after that, after the ice was broken. Then you both came — I was so relieved — and here we are 'just off the yacht !' "

Billy thought it hardly worth while to go to bed when the cab at length reached the Square. He would have preferred to utilise the short time that remained before nine o'clock in talking over his little jaunt with Dilford. He wanted to "shake" John and Haydock, and spend a pleasant hour or two at Mr. Vosler's hotel in town, before meeting his judge. But the plan wasn't one that he could innocently suggest ; and as the senior stayed with them until they said good-night to him at the entry of Matthews, he couldn't very well leave John without a word, as he would

have done, had they been alone.   Billy
tumbled into bed as soon as he got upstairs, and giggled himself to sleep, after
calling into John's room, —

"You did see the sunrise, did n't you,
old man ?"

John lay awake until it was time to
rouse Billy for his trial.   At nine that
morning the two criminals rolled up to
the court-room, smoking cigarettes on the
back seat of a victoria.   They pleaded
guilty to something, — neither of them
quite knew what, — listened with downcast
eyes to a bit of fatherly sarcasm, and
drove away again — forty dollars poorer
than when they arrived.   That was in
January.

The midyear examinations have an unpleasant habit of disturbing the even academic tenor early in February, as their
name suggests.   They announce themselves, in various prominent places, at
first, like clouds no bigger than a man's
hand.   The wary and the wise repair to
their caves, and remain there, off and on,
for days and days and days.   When they
finally emerge, care-worn but preserved
after the deluge, they find that many

loved ones are missing.   John was among
the first to retire to high and inaccessible
altitudes.   He pinned the "Crimson's"
supplementary schedule of examinations
and dates to his door.   After deliberating
long as to where a similar reminder would
most often meet the eyes of his room-mate,
he carefully marked the impending tor-
tures with ominous crosses and tacked the
list to the frame of Billy's mirror.   He
might with just as much effect — to say
nothing of the economy of anguish —
have thrown the thing into the fire.

"What the devil does this fly-paper
think it's doing on my looking-glass?"
Billy had remarked on finding the evi-
dence of John's thoughtfulness.   "Do
you realise that you have utterly obliter-
ated Sarah Bernhardt and Della Fox? I
think you must be crazy."   He ripped
off the paper, and let it flutter to the floor.
John's patience was inexhaustible, but his
ingenuity had well defined limits ; he was
aware, with something like panic, that he
had reached them.   For weeks, he had
exercised what art he had at command, in
trying to seduce Billy into opening a
book.   He had learned that a declaration

of his personal ideas in regard to the examinations — or any work he undertook — was worse than ineffectual as far as his room-mate went. It not only failed to quicken in Billy the sense — prevalent at the midyears — of approaching catastrophe, but drove him away to somebody's else room, or perhaps to town. So, much to his own distaste, John had essayed the rôle of the serio-comic. He made a pretence — with reservations — of adopting Billy's point of view; the reservations were meant to bring about the desired end. He would chat with Billy of the more serious aspects of college — the courses and instructors and examinations — in an attempt at something like the same breezy tone in which the boy himself touched on these subjects. When Billy, for instance, would sit up in bed in the morning and yawn and shrug and announce that he simply could n't go all the way over to Sever Hall to sit through Professor So-and-so's lecture — that the man was ninety-five years old if he was a day, and slobbered, John would laugh and say, —

"Yes, is n't he deadly? I hardly ever

listen to him. Lots of people live too
long. But I suppose we must go and
endure it; we're in the course, and we'll
have to worry through it somehow."

At first Billy was rather shocked. The
abrupt change of manner was so hopelessly out of character; he would n't have
been more astounded had he heard un-
seemly levity issuing from the pulpit at
S. Timothy's. But he divined almost at
once — who would n't have? — that John's
responsibility for other people's affairs,
though exhibited in a fashion positively
weird, did not diminish; and Billy fre-
quented 86 Matthews less than ever.
John knew that he himself did n't possess
the qualities that make a man an inspiration, but he had been brought up at home
and at school to believe that he was something of an influence; that he was "just
the sort of man a fellow like Billy needs."
Apart from the genuine sorrow he would
feel at what the official college gracefully
terms the "separation" of Billy from
the University, it was disconcerting to
John to find out that as a kindly light
he had proved uncommonly dim. In
despair and disappointment, he im-

pressed Haydock into the labour of salvation.

Haydock was very amiable about the whole affair. He had, whenever he was with Billy, the half amused affection an older fellow often feels for anything so young and pretty and inconsequent. He liked the boy's mother too, although the lady's guilelessness had always been a bar to conversation of other than a purely theoretical value. So, in response to John's eleventh-hour prayers, he did what he could in spite of more immediate interests. He picked his way, one evening, through the darkness and the mud, and among the disabled butcher-waggons, by the black alley that leads to the Polo Club, — once upon a time he too had belonged to that genial institution, — and beguiled Billy and Dilford Bancroft to his room. He gave them beer, and things to smoke, and then wondered how, with two such elusive, mercurial creatures flitting about, he could ever begin to " talk shop." Strangely enough Billy himself provided the opportunity.

" Play something, Dilly," he said, opening Haydock's piano. Haydock glanced at the clock on the mantelpiece, but it was not yet nine; the proctor could n't object, no matter how excruciating Dilly's performance might be.

"Dilly, you know, can bang the box in a way that would make you throw stones at your grandmother," explained Billy.

"I'm extremely fond of my grandmother," suggested Haydock.

"What do you want?" asked Dilly, seating himself.

"What do you know?"

"Oh, any old thing."

Haydock was on the point of discreetly asking for a Sousa march, when Dilford plunged abruptly into the middle of a sonata, and played it through with astonishing brilliancy.

"I do play well, don't I?" he admitted, when he had finished. "It always surprises me; just think what I could do if I really studied — hard, I mean," he added lightly.

"Good heavens! man," exclaimed Haydock, "are n't you going to take highest honours in music? Why, you can do anything!" Haydock considered his own little thumpings important only in so far as they enabled him to understand a talent like Bancroft's.

" Oh, I don't know," answered Dilford, with indifference. " My father wants me to go to work; I don't suppose I'll be here long."

" Won't you, really? I knew that Billy was n't going to stay; but I had an idea you would." Haydock alluded to Billy's probable departure with the emotion he would have displayed had he been predicting a change in the weather.

Billy pricked up his ears and his eyebrows at once. " What makes you say that? " he demanded quickly. Even Dilford dropped his customary listlessness, and looked interested.

" Why — I thought it was more or less settled." The senior turned from one to the other in slow surprise, " If I 've said anything I ought not to have — given things away, I mean — I 'm awfully sorry. But perhaps they were mistaken." Billy's face, across which flitted a shade of anxiety, told him that he was perfectly safe in making a " bluff" at changing the subject.

" No, no! " Billy jerked out, impatiently; " go on! who are you talking about? You've heard something important," something that didn't emanate from John, he was thinking. "What did they say? I insist on knowing."

"It really wasn't much; merely that one or two of the instructors — I know some of the younger ones rather well — seemed to think that you would n't — that in fact you could n't be with us after the midyears. That's all. I thought you knew."

"You're bitched all right, all right," laughed Bancroft.

"They said that, did they?" Billy let fall these words portentously; it was as if he were on the point of framing a great resolution.

"That's precisely what they said."

"Well, then — by heaven! I'll fool them." He really meant it.

"Oh, I wish you would! It would be easy after all. There's time yet. I'll help you with your English — both courses — and your Latin. You're all right in French, of course, and the History won't be so terrible. Is it a go?" Haydock held out his hand.

"I'll fool them," repeated Billy, solemnly. He gravely let his long, brown fingers rest in Haydock's palm. And Haydock had one of those moments of quiet exultation that are the perquisites of the intelligent.

The next morning Billy and Dilly disappeared from Cambridge, and were neither seen nor heard of for five days. On the afternoon of the fourth day John, looking positively thin, turned up in Haydock's room.

"Get up a search party and explore darkest Boston," advised the senior, drumming on the desk with his pencil.

"Oh, I did!" John's tone was without hope. "Harry Hollis and Jimmy Fenton took me all over — to the most awful hotels and places. They seemed to know Billy at all of them; but he was n't there. I never had such a night. I don't know what to do."

"How much money did he have?" Haydock continued to drum thoughtfully.

"Twenty dollars. I'm sure, because we both put our allowances in the bank that morning. Billy kept twenty."

Now Haydock, who had met a great number of Billys and Dillys in his short

life, knew that this particular Billy was not
living anywhere on the modest sum of five
dollars a day.   So, after a little more drumming, he said, —

" Run over to the Charles River Bank,
and ask them in just what metropolis of
the United States or Europe, William is
signing cheques at the present moment."

When John returned, breathless, a few
minutes later, he threw himself into a
chair, and groaned, —

" They 're in Providence."

Haydock gave up a dinner at his club
that night, and a dance in town.   He
went, instead, to Providence.   Late the
next evening he deposited Billy — too
much of a wreck to be either resentful or
flippant — in 86 Matthews.   The next
day the Office put Billy " on probation."

And the midyears were coming.

One night, after the examination period
was well under way, Haydock went up to
his room to study.   Although the month
was February, the night was heavy and
depressing.   The senior had much to
accomplish before morning.   He was
nervous — almost irritable.   His curtains
floated like ghostly, beckoning sleeves in

and out of the open windows, until he
jumped up and tied them viciously into
hard knots. His student lamp radiated
the heat of hell and the unnumbered suns ;
he found himself waiting, in nervous sus-
pense, for the periodic bubbling of its
rudimentary bowels. The sound diverted
his attention from his book, and wasted
the limited time left him in which to com-
mit to memory several hundred lines of
Paradise Lost. The verse, —

"And sweet reluctant amourous delay,"

— he came across it in the feverish
scramble of learning five lines a minute by
the watch, — suddenly put the situation in
a light in which he had not until then been
able to see it. He leaned back in his
chair and laughed aloud. And as he
laughed, he heard a light footstep in the
hall, then a knock on his door.

"I heard you laughing and knew you
could n't be working, so I just knocked,"
said Dilford Bancroft, innocently ignoring
the very unusual fact that Haydock had
on neither coat nor waistcoat, that a
shaded student lamp was the only light in
the room, and that several open books

and some scattered notes lay on the table. "What's the joke?" he asked. Then without waiting for an answer, "Hasn't Billy come yet?"

"Is Billy coming?" said Haydock, with an interest that sprang solely from alarm.

"Oh, yes — he'll be here," answered Dilly, reassuring any foolish doubts on that question. He had opened the piano and was striking careful discords in the bass, "I was sure you were talking to him when I came in; he said he'd bring round his system."

"His *what?*"

"Why, his system — the 'Rhyming Road,' he calls it. You're going to give us a seminar, you know — the exam comes to-morrow; and he's going to bring round his notes and the 'Rhyming Road' to help out."

Haydock was hearing of this little arrangement for the first time. He hadn't seen Billy since the return from Providence.

"You didn't tell me you were coming," he began; "I have no end of work myself and —"

"Yes, yes, I know," broke in Dilly, a trifle impatiently, without turning from the piano; "you see we never thought about it ourselves until this afternoon, when we found out that the exam comes to-morrow. We were sure you'd do it," he wheeled slowly about until he faced Haydock; "because neither of us know anything, and if you don't — we'll fail."

Haydock met this plaint with the worried silence of one who dimly foresees his own end. Dilly could n't have made a more persuasive appeal if he had tried. Its strength lay in the fact that Dilly had n't tried; he had simply laid bare, with an apparently childlike trust in Haydock's wisdom, his own and Billy's hopeless inconsequence. It was rather late in the day to discuss the matter.

"We were counting on you," Dilly sighed, and looked at the floor. He ventured this statement in the hope of keeping the subject alive; somehow it had seemed to languish.

"I confess I don't understand you two," Haydock burst out. Every one who had the pleasure of knowing Billy and Dilly took refuge in this exclamation at

one time or another. " How the devil
have you managed to hang on here for
four months? And why on earth did
you come to college at all?" he shook
the boy by the shoulders.

Dilly's apologia might have been interesting. He had on occasions attempted
— by request — to defend the fact of his
being at Harvard; but as he had always
prefaced his few remarks with, " To begin
with, I am of a taciturn disposition," and
as no one was quite willing to believe that
he had a glimmer of the meaning of
" taciturn," he had never been allowed to
proceed from that point. To-night the
appearance of Billy with an armful of
note-books made explanation impossible.

" Oh, I 'm so glad you 're not working," said Billy, sweetly, all the note-books
— there were six of them — fell to the
floor when he sat down; " because we
could n't have disturbed you, and I don't
know what we 'd have done — Dilford's
told you? "

" Yes, Dilford has told me," answered
Haydock. He knew that then was the
time to escort these young gentlemen to
the hall, and lock the door in their faces.

But he allowed it to slip by, and it never
returned.

"Well, then — I don't see why we
should n't dash right along. What do
you think?" Billy looked from Haydock
to Dilford and back again.

"What is it you want — and what are
all those books doing?" Haydock asked
wearily.

"Oh, these?" Billy allowed his feet to
ramble among the volumes on the floor.
"Oh, they 're just notes — History and
French and things; there were no matches
in my room, and I was in a hurry, so I had
to bring them all. The Literature ones
are there too; but they 're rather — rather
— what shall I say?" He refrained
delicately from saying what was the simple
truth, — that his notes on all subjects were
an illegible muddle, beginning nowhere
— arriving nowhere. "Things come to
me at such odd times," he went on, "I
just jot them down. Anyhow you won't
need notes; we merely want you to give
us some idea to go by," he fluttered his
slender hand comprehensively, "an idea
of literature."

"Yes," put in Dilly, stirred by the

practical common sense of the suggestion, "the examination, I think, is about
literature."

"You *think* — good God, child, don't
you *know?*" Haydock mopped his forehead on the back of his arm, and stared at
the two incredulously.

"Oh, he'll catch on all right," said
Billy, easily. "You see the course only
came once a week, and Darnell lectures
so fast that, sitting away in the back of
the room as we do — "

"You prefer, on the whole, to stay
away entirely, or make the hour pass as
rapidly as possible. Yes, yes, I understand," interrupted Haydock, drily. He
picked up one of Billy's books marked
" English 28," and opened it at random,
to a page devoted to the diagrams and
scores of the " Harvard University Tit
Tat Too and Cent Matching Association.
Originators and Sole Proprietors, William Prescott Ware and Dilford Bancroft.
Honorary member: President Eliot." On
the page following was a fragmentary list
of the writers whose lives and achievements
had been taken up in the course. After
the name of Jane Austen, came the an-

nouncement, in parentheses, that "this woman was a man." The startling bit of literary gossip was annotated by: "I was mistaken — it was George Eliot who was a woman."

"That almost flunked me at the hour exam," explained Billy, diffidently. "They 're so fussy about things here." He was looking over Haydock's shoulder. "It would have, I think, if I had n't thrown a new light on the temperament of Swift."

"I 'll warrant you did," said Haydock. "What on earth is this?" The list was followed by page after page of scrappy-looking verse.

"Oh, that 's the Rhyming Road," exclaimed Billy, not without pride. "It sums everything up and helps the memory. See now — I never can forget about that old Eliot woman as long as I live." Haydock followed Billy's guiding finger, and read a stanza that began : —

> "Oh, heavens, oh, heavens,
> Miss Mary Ann Evans,
> Why did you change your name?
> But I 'm on to you, Mary,
> You wary old fairy — "

"And this one on Matthew Arnold," continued Billy, "gives the whole man away at once —"

> "Matthew Arnold — he's all right,
> Full of sweetness, full of light."

"And Richardson —"

> "'Pamela, Pamela, what have you done?'
> 'I've been shooting the chutes with Sir Charles Grandison.'"

"Do you see? It goes on like that, only I haven't had time yet to make the thing complete. Now let's begin; it's late."

Haydock closed the book thoughtfully and went over to the window. He stood a moment looking out at the thick fog, and wondering what he should do. He hadn't the slightest intention any longer of spending the rest of the night in a futile effort to scrape Billy through an examination. The child had already cut two, and failed in one, John had said. But the senior was in doubt as to whether his concern in the mess young Ware had made of his first few months of college,

ought to end there, with a bland "good-
night," or whether he ought to see the
thing out, in — say, the manner in which
he would engineer the calamity, had Billy
happened to be his young brother. A
senior feels toward a freshman, older than
he will ever feel toward anything again —
older, probably, than he will feel even
when called on to give advice to his own
offspring. Haydock realised so well what
was going to happen to Billy — Billy,
whose progress in college from the first,
had been the progress of a flimsy butterfly
in a stiff breeze. He knew to an inch the
quantity of perfectly necessary but distressing red tape that would have to be
measured before Mrs. Ware and the college Office could come to anything like a
common understanding. And even then
Mrs. Ware would n't understand much of
anything. It always seemed to Haydock
that men and women in becoming parents
somehow or other managed to forfeit a
great deal of intelligence. He intended
some day to ask a psychologist with
children, if this was a provision or a per-
version of nature. Mrs. Ware was the
sort of woman who would take an hour

and a half to inform the Dean that William was a "good boy at heart," — that his cheerfulness had always been "a ray of sunshine" in her life ; the Dean, all the while, knowing that the twenty-five young men he had summoned to appear before him that morning, were waiting apprehensively in the outer office to "have it over with." Since there was no question in Haydock's mind just then of how to keep Billy in college, he asked himself if it wouldn't be less painful to every one concerned to get him out with decency and despatch.

"It's late," repeated Dilly, listlessly.

"Yes, that's the trouble," said Haydock, turning away from the window. He said it kindly, regretfully, but with a seriousness that rather alarmed Dilford, and could not be ignored by Billy. "It's too late. There's no use in being tiresome and melo-dramatic about the thing, but that's the simple fact ; you've come to the end of your string, and you've got to let go before they slap your hands and take it away from you. If you don't know what it means, — probation, and cutting two exams, and flunking a third — "

" John told you that," broke in Billy, angrily.

" And flunking again to-morrow, I 'm sorry." He was sorry, very, very sorry. " Because it prolongs the agony for everybody, your mother in particular."

Dilford was sidling about the room, nearing the door by furtive stages. When Haydock glanced up, he was no longer there.

" I 'm the last person in the world to advise running away as long as there's any music to face. But there isn't any more for you just now. The thing is played out, and you simply have to leave." Haydock himself did n't quite know what he meant by this tuneful figure of speech ; but he thought it sounded rather well, and would impress Billy. " You know yourself that a smash of some kind is coming — you 've known it for weeks." The senior did n't attempt to understand the mind in which a keen knowledge of approaching, but easily averted doom ran in a never converging parallel with an insatiable lust for the present. He merely knew that such minds could be, and that Billy's, if left unmolested, was one of them. He

undertook now to lead these lines to a
point. He did n't say very much, and his
remarks were n't in the least spiritual ;
as a matter of fact they were decidedly
worldly. He did n't remind Billy that
his wickedness might eventually keep him
out of the kingdom of Heaven, but told
him, — which is of far more importance to
a Harvard freshman — that if he went on
making an ass of himself he would ruin
his chances for the " Dickey." Haydock
played some variations on this seemingly
simple theme, threw in a few merciless
truths he had learned from John, an original reflection or two, and an unanswerable
prediction of a general and depressing
character.

" You must get out and go home, and
think about it," he ended.

Billy had probably already begun to
act on the last of these suggestions, for in
a minute or two he stuffed his head into
the sofa-cushions and began to cry. Haydock returned to his Milton, and learned
several pages to an accompaniment of
smothered sobs, until Billy at length became quiet.

" Now we 'll go down and have a cool

swim in the tank," said Haydock, rousing him gently. They undressed in silence. Billy was pathetic and absurd in a long blanket wrapper, his face still wet with tears, pattering after Haydock through the halls to the bath.

"Maybe you had better see your 'adviser,'" Haydock suggested, when they were back again in his room. Billy had n't spoken in the interval.

"I can't — he hates me!" gulped Billy, turning away. Ordinarily he would have said that the man was "*affreux.*"

He went to bed and cried some more on the cool pillows. Haydock wrote out a respectful form of resignation from the college for him to copy in the morning, composed a letter to Mrs. Ware, tenderly adapted in all respects to that lady's intellectual needs, and returned, when the fog at his windows was white with the morning, to Paradise Lost.

A DEAD ISSUE

MARCUS THORN, instructor in Harvard University, was thirty-two years old on the twentieth of June. He looked thirty-five, and felt about a hundred. When he got out of bed on his birthday morning, and pattered into the vestibule for his mail, the date at the top of the Crimson recalled the first of these unpleasant truths to him. His mirror — it was one of those detestable folding mirrors in three sections — enabled him to examine his bald spot with pitiless ease, reproduced his profile some forty-five times in quick succession, and made it possible for him to see all the way round himself several times at once. It was this devilish invention that revealed fact number two to Mr. Thorn, while he was brushing his hair and tying his neck-tie. One plus two equalled three, as usual, and Thorn felt old and unhappy. But he did n't linger over his dressing to phi-

losophise on the evanescence of youth ;
he did n't even murmur, —

" Alas for hourly change !   Alas for all
The loves that from his hand proud youth lets fall,
Even as the beads of a told rosary.''

He could do that sort of thing very well ;
he had been doing it steadily for five
months.   But this morning, the reality
of the situation — impressed upon him
by the date of his birth — led him to adopt
more practical measures.   What he actually
did, was to disarrange his hair a little on
top, — fluff it up to make it look more, —
and press it down toward his temples to
remove the appearance of having too much
complexion for the size of his head.
Then he went out to breakfast.

Thorn's birthday had fallen, ironically,
on one of those rainwashed, blue-and-gold
days when " all nature rejoices."   The
whitest of clouds were drifting across the
bluest of skies when the instructor walked
out into the Yard ; the elms rustled gently
in the delicate June haze, and the robins
hopped across the yellow paths, freshly
sanded, and screamed in the sparkling grass.
All nature rejoiced, and in so doing got

very much on Thorn's nerves. When he reached his club, he was a most excellent person not to breakfast with.

It was early — half-past eight — and no one except Prescott, a sophomore, and Wynne, a junior, had dropped in as yet. Wynne, with his spectacles on, was sitting in the chair he always sat in at that hour, reading the morning paper. Thorn knew that he would read it through from beginning to end, carefully put his spectacles back in their case, and then go to the piano and play the " Blue Danube." By that time his eggs and coffee would be served. Wynne did this every morning, and the instructor, who at the beginning of the year had regarded the boy's methodical habits at the club as " quaint," — suggestive, somehow, of the first chapter of " Pendennis," — felt this morning that the " Blue Danube " before breakfast would be in the nature of a last straw. Prescott, looking as fresh and clean as the morning, was laughing over an illustrated funny paper. He merely nodded to Thorn, although the instructor had n't breakfasted there for many months, and called him across to enjoy something.

Thorn glanced at the paper and smiled feebly.

"I don't see how you can do it at this hour," he said; "I would as soon drink flat champagne." Prescott understood but vaguely what the man was talking about, yet he did n't appear disturbed or anxious for enlightenment.

"I 'll have my breakfast on the piazza," Thorn said to the steward who answered his ring. Then he walked nervously out of the room.

From the piazza he could look over a tangled barrier of lilac bushes and trellised grapevines into an old-fashioned garden. A slim lady in a white dress and a broad brimmed hat that hid her face was cutting nasturtiums and humming placidly to herself. Thorn thought she was a young girl, until she turned and revealed the fact that she was not a young girl — that she was about his own age. This seemed to annoy him in much the same way that the robins and Wynne and the funny paper had, for he threw himself into a low steamer-chair where he would n't have to look at the woman, and gave himself up to a sort of luxurious melancholy.

In October, nine months before, Thorn had appeared one evening in the doorway of the club dining-room after a more or less continuous absence of eight years from Cambridge. It was the night before college opened, and the dining-room was crowded. For an instant there was an uproar of confused greetings; then Haydock and Ellis and Sears Wolcott and Wynne — the only ones Thorn knew — pushed back from the table and went forward to shake hands with him. Of the nine or ten boys still left at the table by this proceeding, those whose backs were turned to the new arrival stopped eating and waited without looking around, to be introduced to the owner of the unfamiliar voice. Their companions opposite paused too; some of them laid their napkins on the table. They, however, could glance up and see that the newcomer was a dark man of thirty years or more. They supposed, correctly, that he was an " old graduate " and a member of the club.

"You don't know any of these people, do you?" said Haydock, taking him by the arm; "what a devil of a time you 've been away from this place."

" I know that that's a Prescott,"
laughed the graduate. In his quick survey of the table, while the others had been
welcoming him back, his eyes had rested
a moment on a big fellow with light hair.
Everybody laughed, because it really was
a Prescott and all Prescotts were simply
more or less happy replicas of all other
Prescotts. " I know your brothers," said
the graduate, shaking hands with the boy,
who had risen.

"It's Mr. Thorn." Haydock made
this announcement loud enough to be
heard by the crowd. He introduced
every one, prefixing " Mr." to the names
of the first few, but changing to given and
even nicknames before completing the cir-
cuit of the table. The humour of some
of these last, — " Dink," " Pink," and
" Mary," for instance, — lost sight of in
long established usage, suggested itself
anew; and the fellows laughed again as
they made a place for Thorn at the crowded
table.

"It's six years, isn't it?" Haydock
asked politely. The others had begun
to babble cheerfully again of their own
affairs.

"Six! I wish it were; it's eight," answered Thorn. "Eight since I left college. But of course I've been here two or three times since, — just long enough to make me unhappy at having to go back to Europe again."

"And now you're a great, haughty Ph. D. person, an 'Officer of Instruction and Government,' announced in the prospectus to teach in two courses," mused Ellis, admiringly. "How do you like the idea?"

"It's very good to be back," said Thorn. He looked about the familiar room with a contented smile, while the steward bustled in and out to supply him with the apparatus of dining.

It was, indeed, good to be back. The satisfaction deepened and broadened with every moment. It was good to be again in the town, the house, the room that, during his life abroad, he had grown to look upon more as "home" than any place in the world; good to come back and find that the place had changed so little; good, for instance, when he ordered a bottle of beer, to have it brought to him in his own mug, with his name and

class cut in the pewter, — just as if he
had never been away at all.   This was
but one of innumerable little things that
made Thorn feel that at last he was where
he belonged ; that he had stepped into his
old background ; that it still fitted.   The
fellows, of course, were recent acquisi-
tions — all of them.   Even his four acquaintances had entered college long since
his own time.   But the crowd, except that
it seemed to him a gathering decidedly
younger than his contemporaries had been
at the same age, was in no way strange to
him.   There were the same general types
of young men up and down the table, and
at both ends, that he had known in his
day.   They were discussing the same
topics, in the same tones and inflections,
that had made the dinner-table lively in
the eighties, — which was not surprising
when he considered that certain families
belong to certain clubs at Harvard almost
as a matter of course, and that some of
the boys at the table were the brothers
and cousins of his own classmates.   He
realised, with a glow of sentiment, that he
had returned to his own people after years
of absence in foreign lands ; a perform-

ance whose emotional value was not decreased for Thorn by the conviction, just
then, that his own people were better bred,
and better looking, and better dressed
than any he had met elsewhere. As he
looked about at his civilised surroundings, and took in, from the general chatter,
fragments of talk, — breezy and cosmo-
politan with incidents of the vacation just
ended, — he considered his gratification
worth the time he had been spending
among the fuzzy young gentlemen of a
German university.

Thorn, like many another college an-
tiquity, might have been the occasion of
a mutual feeling of constraint had he
descended upon this undergraduate meal
in the indefinite capacity of "an old graduate." The ease with which he filled his
place at the table, and the effortless civility
that acknowledged his presence there, were
largely due to his never having allowed
his interest in the life of the club to wane
during his years away from it. He knew
the sort of men the place had gone in for,
and, in many instances, their names as well.
Some of his own classmates — glad, no
doubt, of so congenial an item for their

17

occasional European letters — had never failed to write him, in diverting detail, of the great Christmas and spring dinners. And they, in turn, had often read extracts from Thorn's letters to them, when called on to speak at these festivities. More than once the graduate had sent, from the other side of the world, some doggerel verses, a sketch to be used as a dinner-card, or a trifling addition to the club's library or dining-room. Haydock and Ellis and Wolcott and Wynne he had met at various times abroad. He had made a point of hunting them up and getting to know them, with the result that his interest had succeeded in preserving his identity; he was not unknown to the youngest member of the club. If they did n't actually know him, they at least knew of him. Even this crust is sweet to the returned graduate whose age is just far enough removed from either end of life's measure to make it intrinsically unimportant.

"What courses do you give?" It was the big Prescott, sitting opposite, who asked this. The effort involved a change of colour.

"You'd better look out, or you'll have Pink in your class the first thing you know," some one called, in a voice of warning, from the other end of the table.

"Yes; he's on the lookout for snaps," said some one else.

"Then he'd better stay away from my lectures," answered Thorn, smiling across at Prescott, who blushed some more at this sudden convergence of attention on himself. "They say that new instructors always mark hard — just to show off."

"I had you on my list before I knew who you were," announced another. "I thought the course looked interesting; you'll have to let me through."

"Swipe! swipe!" came in a chorus from around the table. This bantering attitude toward his official position pleased Thorn, perhaps, more than anything else. It flattered and reassured him as to the impression his personality made on younger — much younger — men. He almost saw in himself the solution of the perennial problem of "How to bring about a closer sympathy between instructor and student."

After dinner Haydock and Ellis took him from room to room, and showed him

the new table, the new rugs, the new
books, *ex dono* this, that, and the other
member.   In the library he came across
one of his own sketches, prettily framed.
Some of his verses had been carefully
pasted into the club scrap-book.   Ellis
and Haydock turned to his class photograph in the album, and laughed.   It was
not until long afterwards that he wondered
if they had done so because the picture
had not yet begun to lose its hair.   When
they had seen everything from the kitchen
to the attic, they went back to the big
room where the fellows were drinking
their coffee and smoking.   Others had
come in in the interval ; they were condol-
ing gaily with those already arrived, on the
hard luck of having to be in Cambridge
once more.   Thorn stood with his back
to the fireplace, and observed them.

It was anything but a representative
collection of college men.   There were
athletes, it was true, — Prescott was one,
— and men who helped edit the college
papers, and men who stood high in their
studies, and others who did n't stand anywhere, talking and chaffing in that room.
But it was characteristic of the life of the

college that these varied distinctions had
in no way served to bring the fellows together there. That Ellis would, without
doubt, graduate with a *magna*, perhaps a
summa cum laude, was a matter of interest
to no one but Ellis. That Prescott had
played admirable foot-ball on Soldiers'
Field the year before, and would shortly
do it again, made Prescott indispensable to
the Eleven, perhaps, but it did n't in the
least enhance his value to the club. In
fact, it kept him away so much, and sent
him to bed so early, that his skill at the
game was, at times, almost deplored. That
Haydock once in a while contributed
verses of more than ordinary merit to the
" Monthly " and " Advocate " had nearly
kept him out of the club altogether. It
was the one thing against him, — he had
to live it down. On the whole, the club,
like all of the five small clubs at Harvard whose influence is the most powerful, the farthest reaching influence in the
undergraduate life of the place, rather
prided itself in not being a reward for
either the meritorious or the energetic. It
was composed of young men drawn from
the same station in life, the similarity of

whose past associations and experience, in addition to whatever natural attractions they possessed, rendered them mutually agreeable. The system was scarcely broadening, but it was very delightful. And as the graduate stood there watching the fellows — brown and exuberant after the long vacation — come and go, discussing, comparing, or simply fooling, but always frankly absorbed in themselves and one another, he could not help thinking that however much such institutions had helped to enfeeble the class spirit of days gone by, they had a rather exquisite, if less diffusive spirit of their own. He liked the liveliness of the place, the broad, simple terms of intimacy on which every one seemed to be with every one else, the freedom of speech and action. Not that he had any desire to bombard people with sofa-cushions, as Sears Wolcott happened to be doing at that instant, or even to lie on his back in the middle of the centre-table with his head under the lamp, and read the " Transcript," as some one else had done most of the evening ; but he enjoyed the environment that made such things possible and unobjectionable.

"I must make a point of coming here a great deal," reflected Thorn.

The next day college opened. More men enrolled in Thorn's class that afternoon than he thought would be attracted by the subject he was announced to lecture in on that day of the week. Among all the students who straggled, during the hour, into the bare recitation-room at the top of Sever, the only ones whose individualities were distinct enough to impress themselves on Thorn's unpractised memory, were a negro, a stained ivory statuette of a creature from Japan, a middle-aged gentleman with a misplaced trust in the efficacy of a flowing sandy beard for concealing an absence of collar and necktie, Prescott, and Haydock. Prescott surprised him. There was a crowd around the desk when he appeared, and Thorn did n't get a chance to speak to him; but he was pleased to have the boy enrol in his course, — more pleased somehow than if there had been any known intellectual reason for his having done such a thing; more pleased, for instance, than he was when Haydock strolled in a moment or two later, although he knew that the

senior would get from his teachings whatever there was in them.   Haydock was
the last to arrive before the hour ended.
Thorn gathered up his pack of enrolment
cards, and the two left the noisy building
together.

"Prescott enrolled just a minute or two
before you did," said Thorn, as they
walked across the Yard.   He was a vain
man in a quiet way.

"Yes," answered Haydock drily, "he
said your course came at a convenient
hour," he did n't add that, from what he
knew of Prescott, complications might,
under the circumstances, be looked for.

"Shall I see you at dinner?" Thorn
asked before they separated.

"Oh, are you going to eat at the
club?"   Haydock had wondered the
night before how much the man would
frequent the place.

"Why, yes, I thought I would — for a
time at least."   No other arrangement had
ever occurred to Thorn.

"That's good — I'm glad," said the
senior; he asked himself, as he walked
away, why truthful people managed to lie
so easily and so often in the course of a

day. As a matter of fact, he was vaguely
sorry for what Thorn had just told him.
Haydock did n't object to the instructor.
Had his opinion been asked, he would
have said, with truth, that he liked the
man. For Thorn was intelligent, and
what Haydock called "house broken,"
and the two had once spent a pleasant
week together in Germany. It was not
inhospitality, but a disturbed sense of the
fitness of things that made Haydock regret Thorn's apparent intention of becoming so intimate with his juniors. The
instructor's place, Haydock told himself,
was with his academic colleagues, at the
Colonial Club — or wherever it was that
they ate.

Thorn did dine with the undergraduates that night, and on many nights following. It was a privilege he enjoyed for
a time exceedingly. It amused him, and,
after the first few weeks of his new life in
Cambridge, he craved amusement. For
in spite of the work he did for the college
— the preparing and delivering of lectures, the reading and marking of various
written tasks, and the enlightening, during
consultation hours, of long haired, long

winded seekers after truth, whose cold,
insistent passion for the literal almost
crazed him — he was often profoundly
bored. He had not been away from Cambridge long enough to outlive the conviction, acquired in his Freshman year, that
the residents of that suburb would prove
unexhilarating if in a moment of inadver-
tence he should ever chance to meet any
of them. But he had been too long an
exile to retain a very satisfactory grasp on
contemporary Boston. Of course he
hunted up some of his classmates he had
known well. Most of them were men of
affairs in a way that was as yet small
enough to make them seem to Thorn
aggressively full of purpose. They were
all glad to see him. Some of them asked
him to luncheon in town at hours that
proved inconvenient to one living in
Cambridge; some of them had wives, and
asked him to call on them. He did so,
and found them to be nice women. But
this he had suspected before. Two of
his classmates were rich beyond the
dreams of industry. They toiled not, and
might have been diverting if they had n't
— both of them — happened to be un-

speakably dull men. For one reason or
another, he found it impossible to see his
friends often enough to get into any but
a very lame sort of step with their lives.
Thorn's occasional meetings with them
left him melancholy, sceptical as to the
depth of their natures and his own,
cynical as to the worth of college friendships — friendships that had depended, for
their warmth, so entirely on propinquity
— on the occasion. His most absorbing
topics of conversation with the men he
had once known — his closest ties — were
after all issues very trivial and very dead.
Dinner with a classmate he grew to look
on as either suicide, or a post mortem.

It was the club with its fifteen or
twenty undergraduate members that went
far at first toward satisfying his idle
moments. Dead issues, other than the
personal traditions that added colour and
atmosphere to the every day life of the
place, were given no welcome there. The
thrill of the fleeting present was enough.
The life Thorn saw there was, as far as he
could tell, more than complete with the
healthy joy of eating and drinking, of
going to the play, of getting hot and

dirty and tired over athletics, and cool and
clean and hungry again afterwards. The
instructor was entranced by its innocence
— its unconscious contentment. It was
so unlike his own life of recent years, he
told himself; it was so " physical." He
liked to stop at the club late in the winter
afternoons, after a brisk walk on Brattle
Street. There was always a crowd around
the fire at that hour, and no room that he
could remember had ever seemed so full
of warmth and sympathy as the big room
where the fellows sat, at five o'clock on
a winter's day, with the curtains drawn
and the light of the fire flickering up the
dark walls and across the ceiling. He often
dropped in at midnight, or even later.
The place was rarely quite deserted.
Returned " theatre bees " came there to
scramble eggs and drink beer, instead of
tarrying with the mob at the Victoria or
the Adams House. In the chill of
the small hours, a herdic load of boys
from some dance in town would often
stream in to gossip and get warm, or to
give the driver a drink after the long
cold drive across the bridge. And
Thorn, who had not been disposed to

gather up and cling to the dropped
threads of his old interests, who was
not wedded to his work, who was not
sufficient unto himself, enjoyed it all
thoroughly, unreservedly — for a time.

For a time only. For as the winter
wore on, the inevitable happened — or
rather the expected did n't happen, which
is pretty much the same thing after all.
Thorn, observant, analytical, and — where
he himself was not concerned — clever,
grew to know the fellows better than they
knew themselves. Before he had lived
among them three months, he had appreciated their respective temperaments, he
had taken the measure of their ambitions
and limitations, he had catalogued their
likes and dislikes, he had pigeon-holed
their weaknesses and illuminated their
virtues. Day after day, night after night,
consciously and unconsciously, he had observed them in what was probably the
frankest, simplest intercourse of their
lives. And he knew them.

But they did n't know him. Nor did
it ever occur to them that they wanted to
or could. They were not seeking the
maturer companionship Thorn had to

give; they were not seeking much of anything.   They took life as they found it
near at hand, and Thorn was far, very
far away. For them, the niche he occu-
pied could have been filled by any gentleman of thirty-two with a kind interest in
them and an affection for the club.   To
him, they were everything that made the
world, as he knew it just then, interesting
and beautiful.   Youth, energy, cleanli-
ness were the trinity Thorn worshipped.
And they were young, strong, and unde-
filed. Yet, after the first pleasure at being
back had left him, Thorn was not a happy
man, although he had not then begun to
tell himself so.

The seemingly unimportant question
presented by his own name began to
worry him a little as the weeks passed into
months.   First names and the absurd
sounds men had answered to from babyhood were naturally in common use at the
club.   Thorn dropped into the way of
them easily, as a matter of course.   Not
to have done so would, in time, have become impossible. The fellows would have
thought it strange — formal.   Yet the
name of " Marcus " was rarely heard there.

Haydock, once in a while, called him that,
after due premeditation. Sears Wolcott
occasionally used it by way of a joke —
as if he were taking an impertinent liberty,
and rather enjoyed doing it. But none of
the other men ever did. On no occasion
had any one said "Marcus" absent-
mindedly, and then looked embarrassed, as
Thorn had hoped might happen. It hurt
him a little always to be called "Thorn;"
to be appealed to in the capacity of "Mr.
Thorn," as he sometimes was by the
younger members, positively annoyed
him. Prescott was the most incorrigible
in this respect. He had come from one
of those fitting schools where all speech
between master and pupil is carried on to
a monotonous chant of "Yes, sir," "No,
sir," and "I think so, sir." He had ideas,
or rather habits, — for Prescott's ideas
were few, — of deference to those whose
mission it was to assist in his education
that Thorn found almost impossible to
displace. For a long time — until the
graduate laughed and asked him not to
— he prefixed the distasteful "Mr." to
Thorn's name. Then, for as long again,
he refrained markedly from calling him

anything. One afternoon he came into the club where the instructor was alone, writing a letter, and after fussing for a time among the magazines on the table, he managed to say, —

"Thorn, do you know whether Sears has been here since luncheon?"

Thorn did n't know and he did n't care, but had Prescott handed him an appointment to an assistant professor's chair, instead of having robbed him a little of what dignity he possessed, he would not have been so elated by half. Prescott continued to call him "Thorn" after that, but always with apparent effort, — as if aware that in doing it he was not living quite up to his principles. This trouble with his name might have served Thorn as an indication of what his position actually was in the tiny world he longed so much to be part of once more. But he was not a clever man where he himself was concerned.

Little things hurt him constantly without opening his eyes. For instance, it rarely occurred to the fellows that the instructor might care to join them in any of their hastily planned expeditions to town after dinner. Not that he was ostracised; he was simply overlooked. When he did go to the theatre, he bought the tickets himself, and asked Prescott or Sears, or some of them, to go with him. The occasion invariably lacked the charm of spontaneity. When he invited any of them to dine with him in town, as he often did, they went, if they had n't anything else to do, and seemed to enjoy their dinner. But to Thorn these feasts were a series of disappointments. He always got up from the table with a sense of having failed in something. What? He did n't know — he could n't have told. He was like a man who shoots carefully at nothing, and then feels badly because he hits it. He persisted in loitering along sunny lanes, and growing melancholy because they led nowhere. It was Sears Wolcott who took even the zest of anticipation out of Thorn's little dinners in town, by saying to the graduate one evening, —

"What 's the point of going to the Victoria for dinner? It 's less trouble, and a damned sight livelier, to eat out here." Sears had what Haydock called, "that

disagreeable habit of hitting promiscu-
ously from the shoulder." The reaction
on Thorn of all this was at last a dawn-
ing suspicion of his own unimportance.
By the time the midyear examinations
came, he felt somehow as if he were
"losing ground;" he had n't reached the
point yet of realising that he never had
had any. He used to throw down his
work in a fit of depression and consult
his three-sided mirror apprehensively.

The big Prescott, however, became the
real problem, around which the others
were as mere corollaries. It was he who
managed, in his "artless Japanese way,"
as the fellows used to call it, to crystallise
the situation, to bring it to a pass where
Thorn's rather unmanly sentimentality
found itself confronted by something
more definite and disturbing than merely
the vanishing point of youth. Prescott
accomplished this very simply, by doing
the poorest kind of work — no work at
all, in fact — in the course he was taking
from Thorn. Barely, and by the grace
of the instructor, had he scraped through
the first examination in November. Since
then he had rested calmly, like a great

monolith, on his laurels. He went to
Thorn's lectures only after intervals of
absence that made his going at all a farce.
He ignored the written work of the course,
and the reports on outside reading, with
magnificent completeness. Altogether, he
behaved as he would n't have behaved had
he ever for a moment considered Thorn
in any light other than that of an instructor, an officer of the college, a creature to whom deference — servility, almost
— was due when he was compelled to talk
to him, but to whom all obligation ended
there. His attitude was not an unusual
one among college "men" who have not
outgrown the school idea, but the atten-
dant circumstances were. For Thorn's
concern over Prescott's indifference to the
course was aroused by a strong personal
attachment, one in which an ordinary
professorial interest had nothing to do.
He smarted at his failure to attract the
boy sufficiently to draw him to his lectures; yet he looked with a sort of panic
toward the ¦approaching day when he
should be obliged, in all conscience, to
flunk him in the midyear examination.
He admired Prescott, as little, intelligent

men sometimes do admire big, stupid ones. He idealised him, and even went the length, one afternoon when taking a walk with Haydock, of telling the senior that under Prescott's restful, olympic exterior he thought there lurked a soul. To which Haydock had answered with asperity, "Well, I hope so, I'm sure," and let the subject drop. Later in the walk, Haydock announced, irrelevantly, and with a good deal of vigour, that if he ever made or inherited millions, he would establish a chair in the university, call it the "Haydock Professorship of Common Sense," and respectfully suggest to the President and Faculty that the course be made compulsory.

Thorn would have spoken to the soulful Prescott, — told him gently that he did n't seem to be quite in sympathy with the work of the course, — if Prescott had condescended to go to his lectures in the six or seven weeks between the end of the Christmas recess and the examination period. But Prescott cut Tuesday, Thursday, and Saturday, at half-past two o'clock, with a regularity that, considered as regularity, was admirable. Toward the last, he did drop in every now and then, sit near the door, and slip out again before the hour was ended. This was just after he had been summoned by the Recorder to the Office for " cutting." Thorn never got a chance to speak to him. He might have approached the boy at the club ; but the instructor shrank from taking advantage of his connection with that place to make a delicate official duty possible. He had all along avoided " shop " there so elaborately, — had made so light of it when the subject had come up, — that he couldn't bring himself at that late day to arise, viper like, from the hearthstone and smite. A note of warning would have had to be light, facetious, and consequently without value, in order not to prove a very false and uncalled for note indeed. The ready coöperation of the Dean, Thorn refrained from calling on ; he was far from wishing to get Prescott into difficulties.

By the time the examination day arrived, the instructor was in a state of turmoil that in ordinary circumstances would have been excessive and absurd. In the case of Thorn, it was half pathetic, half contemptible. He knew that in spite of

Prescott's soul (a superabundance of soul
is, as a matter of fact, a positive hindrance
in passing examinations), the boy would
do wretchedly. To give him an E — the
lowest possible mark, always excepting, of
course, the jocose and sarcastic F — would
be to bring upon himself Prescott's ever-
lasting anger and " despision." Of this
Thorn was sure. Furthermore, the mark
would not tend to make the instructor
wildly popular at the club ; for although
everybody was willing to concede that
Prescott was not a person of brilliant mental attainments, he was very much beloved.
One hears a good deal about the " rough
justice of boys." Thorn knew that such
a thing existed, and did not doubt but
that, in theory, he would be upheld by the
members of the club if he gave Prescott
an E, and brought the heavy hand of the
Office down on him. But the justice of
boys, he reflected, was, after all, rough ; it
would acknowledge his right to flunk
Prescott, perhaps, and, without doubt, hate
him cordially for doing it. Thorn's aver-
sion to being hated was almost morbid.

If, on the other hand, he let the boy
through, — gave him, say, the undeserved

and highly respectable mark of C, —
well, that would be tampering dishonestly
with the standards of the college, gross
injustice to the rest of the students, in-
jurious to the self-respect of the instructor,
and a great many other objectionable
things, too numerous to mention. Altogether, Thorn was in a "state of mind."
He began to understand something of the
fine line that separates instructor from
instructed, on whose other side neither
may trespass.

When at length the morning of the
examination had come and gone, and
Thorn was in his own room at his desk
with the neat bundle of blue-covered books
before him, in which the examinations are
written, it was easy enough to make up
his mind. He knew that the question of
flunking or passing Prescott admitted of
no arguments whatever. The boy's work
in the course failed to present the tiniest
loophole in the way of "extenuating circumstances," and Prescott had capped the
climax of his past record that morning by
staying in the examination-room just an
hour and a quarter of the three hours he
was supposed to be there. That alone

was equivalent to failure in a man of Prescott's denseness. Not to give Prescott a simple and unadorned E would be holding the pettiest of personal interests higher than one's duty to the college. There was no other way of looking at it. And Thorn, whose mind was perfectly clear on this point, deliberately extricated Prescott's book from the blue pile on his desk, dropped it carelessly — without opening it — into the glowing coals of his fireplace, and entered the boy's midyear mark in the records as C.

No lectures are given in the college during the midyears. Men who are fortunate enough to finish their examinations early in the period can run away to New York, to the country, to Old Point Comfort, to almost anywhere that is n't Cambridge, and recuperate. Haydock went South. Ellis and Wynne tried a walking trip in the Berkshire Hills, and, after two days' floundering in the mud, waded to the nearest train for a city. Boston men went to Boston — except Sears Wolcott and Prescott, who disappeared to some wild and inaccessible New England hamlet to snow-shoe or spear fish or shoot

rabbits; no one could with authority say
which, as the two had veiled their prepa-
rations in mystery.   So it happened that
Thorn did n't see Prescott for more than
a week after he had marked his book.
In the mean time he had become used to
the idea of having done it according to
to a somewhat unconventional system—
to put it charitably.   He passed much of
the time in which the fellows were away,
alone ; for the few who went to the club,
went there with note-books under their
arms and preoccupied expressions in their
eyes.   They kept a sharp look-out for
unexpected manœuvres on the part of the
clock, and had a general air of having to
be in some place else very soon.   Thorn,
thrown on his own resources, had a mild
experience of what Cambridge can be
without a crowd to play with, and came
to the conclusion that, for his own interest
and pleasure in life, he had done wisely
in not incurring Prescott's ill-will and
startling the club in the new rôle of hard-
hearted, uncompromising pedagogue.   The
insignificant part he played in the lives of
the undergraduates was far from satisfying ;
but it was the sort of half a loaf one does n't

willingly throw away.   By the time Prescott came back, Thorn had so wholly accepted his own view of the case that he
was totally unprepared for the way in which
the boy took the news of his mark.   He
met Prescott in the Yard the morning college opened again, and stopped to speak
to him.   He would n't have referred to
the examination — it was enough to know
that the little crisis had passed — had not
Prescott, blushing uneasily, and looking
over Thorn's shoulder at something across
the Yard, said, —

"I don't suppose you were very much
surprised at the way I did in the exam,
were you?"

"It might have been better," answered
Thorn, seriously.   "I hope you will do
better the second half year.   But then,
it might have been worse; your mark
was C."

Prescott looked at him, a quizzical,
startled look; and then realising that
Thorn was serious, that there had been
nothing of the sarcastic in his tone or
manner, he laughed rudely in the instructor's face.

"I beg your pardon," he said, as po-

litely as he could, with his eyes still full
of wonder and laughter; " I had no idea
I did so well." He turned abruptly and
walked away. Thorn would have felt
offended, if he had n't all at once been
exceedingly scared. Prescott's manner
was extraordinary for one who, as a rule,
took everything as it came, calmly, unquestioningly. His face and his laugh
had expressed anything but ordinary satisfaction at not having failed. There was
something behind that unwonted astonishment, something more than mere surprise at having received what was, after
all, a mediocre mark. Thorn had mixed
enough with human kind to be aware that
no man living is ever very much surprised
in his heart of hearts to have his humble
efforts in any direction given grade C.
Men like Prescott, who know but little
of the subjects they are examined in, usually try to compose vague answers that
may, like the oracles, be interpreted
according to the mood of him who reads
them. No matter how general or how few
Prescott's answers had been— Thorn
stopped suddenly in the middle of the
path. The explanation that had come to

him took hold of him, and like a tight-
ened rein drew him up short. Prescott
had written nothing. The pages of his
blue book had left the examination-room
as virgin white as when they had been
brought in and placed on the desk by the
proctor. There was no other explanation
possible, and the instructor tingled all
over with the horrid sensation of being
an unspeakable fool. He turned quickly
to go to University Hall; he meant to
have Prescott's mark changed at once.
But Prescott, at that moment, was bound-
ing up the steps of University, two at a
time. He was undoubtedly on his way
to the Office to verify what Thorn had
just told him. Thorn walked rapidly to
his entry in Holworthy, although he had
just come from there. Then, with short,
nervous steps, he turned back again, left
the Yard, and hurried in aimless haste up
North Avenue. He had been an ass, — a
bungling, awful ass, — he told himself over
and over again. And that was about as
coherent a meditation as Mr. Thorn was
able to indulge in for some time. Once
the idea of pretending that he had made a
mistake did suggest itself for a moment;

but that struck him as wild, impossible. It would have merely resulted in forcing the Office to regard him as stupid and careless, and, should embarrassing questions arise, he no longer had Prescott's book with which to clear himself. More than that, it would give Prescott reason to believe him an underhand trickster. The boy now knew him to be an example of brazen partiality; there was no point in incurring even harsher criticism. Thorn tried to convince himself, as he hurried along the straight, hideous highway, that perhaps he was wrong, — that Prescott had n't handed in a perfectly blank book. If only he could have been sure of that, he would have risked the bland assertion that the boy had stumbled on more or less intelligent answers to the examination questions, without perhaps knowing it himself. This, practically, was the tone he had meant to adopt all along. But he could n't be sure, and, unfortunately, the only person who could give information as to what was or was n't in the book, was Prescott. But Prescott had given information of the most direct and convincing kind. That astounded

look and impertinent laugh had as much
as said : —

"Well, old swipe, what's your little
game? What do you expect to get by
giving a good mark to a man who was n't
able to answer a single question?" And
Thorn knew it. At first he was alarmed
at what he had done. He could easily
see how such a performance, if known,
might stand in the light of his reappoint-
ment to teach in the college, even if it
did n't eject him at once. But before he
returned to his room, after walking miles,
he scarcely knew where, fear had entirely
given way to shame, — an over-powering
shame that actually made the man sick at
his stomach. It was n't as if he had com-
mitted a man's fault in a world of men
where he would be comfortably judged and
damned by a tribunal he respected about
as much as he respected himself. He had
turned himself inside out before the clear
eyes of a lot of boys, whose dealings with
themselves and one another were like so
many shafts of white light in an unrefract-
ing medium. He had let them know
what a weak, characterless, poor thing he
was, by holding himself open to a bribe,

showing himself willing to exchange, for
the leavings of their friendships, something he was bound in honour to give
only when earned, prostituting his profes-
sion that they might continue to like him
a little, tolerate his presence among them.
And he was one whom the college had
honoured by judging worthy to stand up
before young men and teach them. It
was really very sickening.

Thorn could n't bring himself to go
near the club for some days. He knew,
however, as well as if he had been present,
what had probably happened there in the
meanwhile. Prescott had told Haydock
and Wolcott, and very likely some of the
others, the story of his examination.
They had laughed at first, as if it had
been a good joke in which Prescott had
come out decidedly ahead ; then Haydock
had said something — Thorn could hear
him saying it — that put the matter in a
pitilessly true light, and the others had
agreed with him. They usually did in
the end. It took all the " nerve " Thorn
had to show himself again.

But when he had summoned up enough
courage to drop in at the club late one

evening, he found every one's manner
toward him pretty much as it always had
been; yet he could tell instinctively, as he
sat there, who had and who had n't heard
Prescott's little anecdote. Wolcott knew;
he called Thorn, "Marcus," with unnecessary gusto, and once or twice laughed his
peculiarly irritating laugh when there was
nothing, as far as Thorn could see, to
laugh at. Haydock knew; Thorn winced
under the cool speculative stare of the
senior's grey eyes. Wynne knew; although Thorn had no more specific reason
for believing so, than that the boy seemed
rather more formidably bespectacled than
usual. Several of the younger fellows
also knew; Thorn knew that they knew;
he could n't stand it. When the front
door slammed after him on his way back
to his room, he told himself that, as far
as he was concerned, it had slammed for
the last time.

He was very nearly right. He would
have had to be a pachyderm compared to
which the "blood sweating behemoth of
Holy Writ" is a mere satin-skinned
invalid, in order to have brazened out the
rest of the year on the old basis. He

could n't go to the club and converse on base-ball and the "musical glasses," knowing that the fellows with whom he was talking were probably weighing the pros and cons of taking his courses next year, and getting creditable marks in them, without doing a stroke of work. He could n't face that "rough justice of boys" that would sanction the fellows making use of him, and considering him a pretty poor thing, at the same time. So he stayed away; he did n't go near the place through March and April and May. When his work did n't call him elsewhere, he stayed in his room and attempted to live the life of a scholar, — an existence for which he was in every conceivable way unfitted. For a time he studied hard out of books; but the most profitable knowledge he acquired in his solitude was the great deal he learned about himself. He tried to write. He had always thought it in him to "write something," if he ever should find the necessary leisure. But the play he began amounted to no more than a harmless pretext for discoursing in a disillusioned strain on Life and Art in the many letters

he wrote to people he had known abroad,
— people, for whom, all at once, he con-
ceived a feeling of intimacy that no doubt
surprised them when they received his
letters. His volume of essays was never
actually written, but the fact that he was
hard at work on it served well as an
answer to : —

"Why the devil don't we ever see you
at the club nowadays?"

For the fellows asked him that, of
course, when he met them in the Yard or
in the electric cars; and Haydock tarried
once or twice after his lecture and hoped
politely that he was coming to the next
club dinner. He was n't at the next club
dinner, however, nor the next, nor the
next. Haydock stopped reminding him
of them. The club had gradually ceased
to have any but a spectacular interest for
Thorn. His part at a dinner there would
be — and, since his return, always had
been — that of decorous audience in the
stalls, watching a sprightly farce. The
club did n't insist on an audience, so
Thorn's meetings with its members were
few. He saw Haydock and Prescott, in a
purely official way, more than any of

them. Strangely enough, Prescott seemed
to be trying to do better in Thorn's
course. He came to the lectures as regu-
larly as he had avoided them before the
midyears. He handed in written work
of such ingenious unintelligence that there
was no question in Thorn's mind as to
the boy's having conscientiously evolved it
unaided. The instructor liked the spirit
of Prescott's efforts, although it was a per-
petual " rubbing in," of the memory of
his own indiscretion ; it displayed a pretty
understanding of *noblesse oblige*.

The second half year was long and
dreary and good for Thorn. It set him
down hard, — so hard that when he col-
lected himself and began to look about
him once more, he knew precisely where
he was — which was something he had n't
known until then. He was thirty-two
years old ; he looked thirty-five, and he
felt a hundred, to begin with. He was n't
an undergraduate, and he had n't been
one for a good many years. He still felt
that he loved youth and sympathised with
its every phase, — from its mindless gam-
bolings to its preposterous maturity.
But he knew now that it was with the

love and sympathy of one who had lost
it. He had learned, too, that when it
goes, it bids one a cavalier adieu, and takes
with it what one has come to regard as
one's rights, — like a saucy house-maid
departing with the spoons. He knew
that he had no rights; he had forfeited
them by losing some of his hair. He
would n't get any of them back again
until he had lost all of it. He was the
merest speck on the horizon of the fellows whom he had, earlier in the year,
tried to know on a basis of equality, — a
speck too far away, too microscopic even
to annoy them. If he had only known
it all along, he told himself, how different his year might have been. He
would n't have squandered the first four
months of it, for one thing, in a stupid
insistence on a relation that must of
necessity be artificial — unsatisfying. He
would n't have spent the last five of it
in coming to his senses. He would n't
have misused all of it in burning — or
at least in allowing to fall into a precari-
ous state of unrepair — the bridges that
led back to the friends of his own age
and time.

"I have learned more than I have taught, this year," thought Thorn.

To-day was Thorn's birthday. Impelled by a tender, tepid feeling of self-pity the instructor had come once more to the club to look at it and say good-bye before leaving Cambridge. He would have liked to breakfast on the piazza and suffer luxuriously alone. But just at the moment he was beginning to feel most deeply, Sears Wolcott appeared at the open French window, and said he was "Going to eat out there in the landscape too." So Thorn, in spite of himself, had to revive.

"What did you think of the Pudding show last night?" began Sears. Talk with him usually meant leading questions and their simplest answers.

"It was very amusing — very well done," said Thorn. What was the use, he asked himself, of drawing a cow-eyed stare from Wolcott by saying what he really thought — that Strawberry Night at the Pudding had been "exuberant," "noisy," "intensely young."

"I saw you after it was over," Sears

went on; "why did n't you buck up with the old grads around the piano? You looked lonely."

" I was lonely," answered Thorn, truthfully this time.

" Where were your classmates? There was a big crowd out."

" My classmates? Oh, they were there, I suppose. I have n't seen much of them this year."

Wolcott's next question was : —

" Why the devil can't we have better strawberries at this club, I wonder? Where's the granulated sugar? They know I never eat this damned face powder on anything." He called loudly for the steward, and Thorn went on with his breakfast in silence. After Sears had been appeased with granulated sugar, he asked : —

" Going to be here next year? "

" I 've been reappointed; but I think I shall live in town. Why do you ask? "

" Oh, nothing — I was thinking I might take your courses. What mark is Prescott going to get for the year? "

Thorn looked up to meet Wolcott's eyes unflinchingly; but the boy was deeply absorbed in studying the little air bubbles on the surface of his coffee.

" I don't know what mark he'll get. I have n't looked at his book yet," said Thorn. Sears remarked " Oh ! " and laughed as he submerged the bubbles with a spoon. It was unlike him not to have said, " You do go through the formality of reading his books then ? "

Prescott and Wynne joined them. They chattered gaily with Wolcott about nothing out there on the piazza, and watched the slim lady on the other side of the nodding lilac bushes cut nasturtiums. Thorn listened to them, and looked at them, and liked them ; but he could n't be one of them, even for the moment. He could n't babble unpremeditatedly about nothing, because he had forgotten how it was done. So, in a little while, he got up to leave them. He had to mark some examination books and pack his trunks and go abroad, he told them. He said good-bye to Prescott and Wolcott and Wynne and some others who had come in while they were at breakfast, and hoped they would have " a good summer." They hoped the same to him.

As he strolled back to his room with the sounds of their voices in his ears, but with no memory of what they had been saying, he wondered if, after all, they had n't from the very first bored him just a little; if his unhappiness — his sense of failure when he talked to young people — did n't come from the fact that they commended themselves to his affections rather than to his intellect.   Thorn was a vain man in a quiet way.

Prescott's final examination book certainly did n't commend itself to his intellect.   It was long, and conscientious, and quite incorrect from cover to cover.   The instructor left it until the last.   He almost missed his train in deciding upon its mark.

THE CLASS DAY IDYL

OF course there is no such thing as the "typical Harvard man," although it interests — or irritates — people who did n't go to Harvard to believe every now and then that they have discovered him. If a well-dressed youth with a broad A, and an abnormal ignorance of the life practical, appears in a Western town, the business man from whom he seeks employment, after sounding the profoundest depths of his incapacity, amuses the family circle at dinner by telling of the call he had from a "typical Harvard man." If a girl sits out a dance with a fellow who does n't give her the look of a slightly bewildered cow when she slings a little Swinburne at him, but who lets fly the tail end of a Rossetti sonnet in return, closely followed by a gem or two purloined here and there from Henry James, she thinks she has met another of those "typical Harvard men." The young American travelling abroad who displays a decent

reticence when compatriots of whom he
never has heard, " put their paws on his
shoulders and lap his face," is described
in many terms — that of " the typical Harvard man " coming last. This strange,
mythical being is all things to all men —
who are not Harvard men; but it is
worthy of note that in the various aspects
in which he is apperceived, he manages to
repeat certain distinguished traits that even
the enemy is bound — often secretly — to
admire. No one, for instance, marks as
typical of Harvard, a man who is ill-
dressed, or ill-bred; he is usually good
looking. So if the typical Harvard man,
like the sea-serpent, continues to agitate
the provinces from time to time, one is
thankful that whatever his disguise may
be for the moment, he is always a distinctly
presentable young person.

Beverly Beverly of the graduating class
was often thought by outsiders to be of
the type to which most Harvard men
belonged. He was a very well arranged
young gentleman who wore glasses. He
always seemed to have plenty of money;
he lived on the ground floor of Beck
Hall, and had a servant.

He lived in Beck rather than in Claverly, because, for some reason or other, Beck is not annually overrun by a crowd of sporty freshmen just released from high-church fitting-schools. Furthermore, although surrounded in Beck by fellow-students whom he felt it possible to know, he didn't happen to know any of them more intimately than a polite nod of the head would imply. So when he retired to his own room he was spared the nocturnal visitations and talk-to-deaths of a more populous building.

Beverly was intelligent, reserved, and "set in his ways." He had been in a great many places, and had met a great many people. By the end of his senior year he preferred to spend his time in doing nothing at all, rather than in doing something that didn't interest him exceedingly. As he had gone to Harvard, people said he was a typical product of that institution. They couldn't have said this if his father had seen fit to send him to a business college to learn how to audit accounts, and make an American eagle with a fist full of thunderbolts in two pen-strokes. But Beverly would have been very much the same sort of person after all, only perhaps not as agreeable as he actually was.

Early in his college career, Beverly had identified himself with the few fellows he cared to know. Since then, his little circle of intimate friends had, if anything, become smaller.

When Class Day — his Class Day — began to be talked about, Beverly, as a matter of course, was asked to spread at Beck. His decision not to spread there — nor anywhere — was as much a matter of course. He did n't enjoy Class Day, he said; it was always unbearably warm; it was impossible on that day to procure nourishment that was n't fluid or semi-fluid, — punch, chicken-salad, or ice-cream; and the vast armies of women, from Heaven knows where, who came early and stayed until they were put out, managed to kill the sentiment of the day for him, he said, even as they exterminated the grass in the College Yard.

"I sha'n't even be in Cambridge," Beverly declared at breakfast, the morning before the great day.

"You really ought to have spread,

you know," said Billy Fields. "It's the only way we have of being nice to people in town who've been nice to us."

"You forget that Bevy considers himself perfectly square with everybody. He went to their entertainments," said Haydock.

"The truth of the matter is, Bevy's afraid somebody will propose to him, and he is too polite to refuse. Those Boston girls are so impulsive!" suggested Wynne.

"Maybe he wouldn't look well in a cap and gown," added another.

"It's foolish not to go to Class Day," said Prescott, for whom the universe was conveniently divided into things that were "foolish" and things that weren't.

"He's afraid that if he stays, he might be bored," chimed in Haydock, again. "Somebody might ask him whether college men didn't have a 'perfectly lovely time,' and which building Austin Hall was. Of course he doesn't know."

"I don't," admitted Beverly, serenely.

"He'd rather sit in his own room on a dais all day, and have Michael fan him, while three black slaves at his feet try to guess the secret of his ennui," continued

Haydock. "Own up, Bevy — are n't you afraid of being bored?"

"Why, of course," answered Beverly. "That's my constant fear ; and you idiots sometimes make me think that it is n't an altogether groundless one."

"To what do we owe the honour of your presence at breakfast this morning?" asked Wynne, bowing low. Beverly usually breakfasted at ten. It was then half-past eight.

"To an examination in pre-Christian Hebrew literature, — nothing else I assure you." Beverly did n't look up from the morning paper he was trying to read.

"And we 're just a little peevish at having to stay for it, instead of getting away five days earlier — are n't we?"

To this Beverly paid no attention whatever, but rang for the steward and asked him to telephone to Foster to send round Lloyd the cabman at once. It looked like rain, and Beverly's examination that morning was over in the Museum — at least a quarter of a mile away. Billy Fields listened to the order, and then called out : —

"Oh, I say there, look out for Beverly Beverly ; he's horribly haughty this morning, ha, ha !" Billy could exaggerate Beverly's accent, and sound startlingly like the original. He could also imitate his "Who the devil are you?" expression and his walk. These things he proceeded to do around the breakfast-table and out into the hall, until the front door slammed behind him. He lingered on the street outside in order to stand in the gutter and salute when Beverly drove away in his cab.

Beverly had watched Billy's little performance with dispassionate interest, and remarked before returning to his newspaper : —

"He's really talented, in a singularly offensive way." But the words sounded amiable rather than otherwise, for, on the whole, Beverly liked to be teased by the fellows. Some of them were clever at it — Billy especially. It pleased Beverly to think it was the little penalty he paid for being mature enough to know definitely what did and did n't amuse him, and to act accordingly. He was sincere in his dislike of Class Day, and did n't

intend to go near it. He objected to
having the Yard enclosed in Christmas-
trees and festooned with paper lanterns, —
to its "pretending to be a beer garden
with Hamlet left out." He considered it
undignified to throw open the University
to a rabble of women, to invite them to
"kick up their heels" in Memorial Hall,
and see them described in the evening
papers as "Harvard's Fair Invaders."
During breakfast, he enlarged on these
views to a scornful audience that finally
arose in its might, tore off his necktie,
ruined his coiffure, threw him out of the
club into his cab, and then retreated and
locked itself in. Even this did n't make
Beverly really angry, he was used to differences of opinion followed by popular
uprisings.

He had intended to say good-bye to
Cambridge the next morning, and take the
one-o'clock train for New York. But
the next morning, after breakfasting at the
Holly Tree, — there is no place else to
breakfast on Class Day except the Oak
Grove, and Beverly disliked the high
stools of that place and the condescend-
ing services of the dethroned empresses

who wait on one there, — he found it was too late to catch the one o'clock without more effort than he was able to make on so warm a day. So, in a moment of tolerance induced perhaps by the realisation that this was, after all, "good-bye," he strolled over to the Yard.

The exercises in Sanders Theatre had just ended, and the "fair invaders" were beginning to invade by the hundreds. They streamed in brilliant procession along the walks, and swarmed over the shady lawns, — glorified groups of summer millinery, trailing after them the pale pink odour of sachet powder and blond hair. They took possession of the parapet of Matthews, the chairs and benches and doorsteps in front of Hollis and Stoughton and Holworthy, stretching the length of the Yard in a many coloured border that resembled the horticultural orgies of the Public Garden. Celestial companies of maidens in diaphanous drapery floated past Beverly, in the wake of panting but determined ladies richly upholstered.

> " 'On, on to the Pudding spread,
> My daughters must be — shall be fed,' "

20

the leaders seemed to say, as they elbowed through the crowd at the exit.   Seniors in fluttering gowns and wilted collars, with proud mothers and satisfied fathers and eager sisters and observant aunts, seniors with one another, and lonely, unattached seniors Beverly had never seen before, who looked as if they did n't quite know whether they were enjoying themselves or not, sauntered by, mopping their foreheads.   The Yard was alive, not with the customary sprinkling of business-like young men hastening, note-book in hand, to lectures, but with a riot of colour, a swishing of skirts, a vague, babbling gaiety that rose in places to an acute trebleness.   And there was the smell of festivity in the hot air, — a smell of pine branches and Chinese lanterns.

Beverly walked once around the Yard, staring severely at the various factors of the gigantic picnic, and was passing Matthews on his way out, when a sudden gust of wind blew a newspaper from the lap of a woman seated on the steps of the building. He strolled after it until it stopped flapping over the grass, picked it up, and, hat

in hand, returned it to its owner. He
had no difficulty in identifying the lady,
although she was one of many resting on
the steps, for she waved the remaining
sheets of the paper at him as he approached, and smiled largely.

"I never was so embarrassed," she
declared, beaming up at him.

"There is no need to be, I assure
you," said Beverly, with a little bow.

"Oh, but I am — you know I am,"
she continued archly. Beverly would have
walked on, had not the strange woman
suddenly leaned forward, — still looking
up at him, — with the air of one about to
impart a confidence. The action would
have made retreat at that moment rather
rude, or at least abrupt, so the senior hesitated deferentially, and returned her look
by one of inquiry.

She was a stout, middle-aged woman
with short, curly, dark hair. Her up-
turned face was round, red, unlined, and
perspiring. She wore a black-satin skirt
under which Beverly could see her low
shoes of yellow leather resting firmly, with
their toes well turned out, on the step
below. Where black skirt and white

linen shirt-waist met, a crimson belt cir-
cumscribed her buxomness as with a band
of flame.   Under one of her chins perched
a crimson cravat of another shade ; and a
crimson ribbon repeated the note in a tiny
sailor hat that was almost upside down
with coquetry.   On her lap lay a red fan
of the circular kind that appears and
disappears at the pull of a silken cord.
Beverly considered her absurd.

"I just know you're a Harvard man,"
she said engagingly. "Now aren't you?"

"Yes, I am," admitted Beverly.

"Oh, I'm so glad!" she clapped her
hands with all the glee of a little girl of
fifty.   "You can help me — you can
explain everything; the newspapers take
so much for granted."   Beverly looked
a trifle wild.

"Now here's a Yard ticket," she fum-
bled a moment among black-satin intricacies, "and here's a Tree ticket, and here's
one for Memorial Hall.   I have an invitation for Beck Hall, too," she added,
drawing out some envelopes.   "Oh, and
this is my ticket to Poughkeepsie!"   She
unfolded a long strip of green pasteboard.
"I'm going to be at that race; oh, I'm

going to be there! You see — I'm a regular Harvard girl."

"And what can I do for you?" asked Beverly, politely.

"I hate to trouble you," she said, almost diffidently; "but I'm so afraid of missing something. If you would explain the tickets to me — tell me of the gates to which they are the key; if you would be so good — and I know you will be. *Ah —je connais mes âmes.*" Her eyelids fluttered up, then down. She pressed the tickets into Beverly's hand. The senior, somewhat astonished, explained their respective uses as rapidly as possible.

"And now the invitation to Beck Hall; you've forgotten that," she said, with a little side glance of reproach.

"Why, it's just an invitation to a spread, — a sort of garden party. You go there any time after the Tree exercises," explained Beverly.

"Ah — but that's not all," said the lady.

"If she only wouldn't look at me that way," thought Beverly.

"I have a cousin," she went on, "the dearest boy in all the world. Look —

this is he." Beverly, with a slight feeling of apprehension, followed her stubby finger down the first column of names engraved on the invitation, until it stopped at "William Paxton Fields."

"Do you know him?" she asked. Beverly wavered a moment; he felt what was coming.

"Yes, I know Fields," he said, restraining a panic-stricken impulse to dart away in the crowd.

"I felt that you did — something told me. He's a dear boy, is n't he?"

"He's a very good fellow," replied Beverly.

"Ah, I like that," she said heartily, straightening her dumpy shoulders and expanding her chest with enthusiasm. "I love the way you great, loyal college men stand up for each other. It's beautiful. Now I must find him," she went on rapidly, with a keen sense of opportunity, "and tell him I'm here — give myself over to him. He lives — where does he live?" For his own sake, Beverly would have cheerfully told her that he did n't know, or that Billy had moved, or that he did n't have a room at all; but he hesitated to separate Billy from his family, when a word might unite them, so he said : —

"He rooms in Claverly Hall; but I doubt if you can find him there now."

"But we can try," she exclaimed with eager optimism. "Which is Claverly?" she looked blandly up and down the Yard.

"It isn't here; it's down there on Mt. Auburn Street." Beverly indicated the direction.

"Not on the 'campus'? Oh, dear!" said Billy's cousin. There was dismay in her tone and on her broad disc of a face.

"No; but it's very easy to find. Anybody will show you," Beverly answered. He thought it was an excellent moment in which to bow himself away.

"Anybody?" she said softly, transfixing him with one of her oblique leers. She was a terribly arch woman.

Her kinship with Fields, and the assumable respectability that went with it, together with her abandoned trust in Harvard chivalry, didn't make her any less awful in Beverly's eyes. They were merely the complement of her already well-developed

genius for imposition ; they made her impossible to evade, — a something inevitable.

"I'm sure he won't be there now,"
repeated Beverly, helplessly.   "We're all
so busy to-day ; we haven't a moment
to ourselves," he added furtively.

"Yes, yes, I know," assented Billy's
cousin ; "but it's my only way to find him
before evening.   I can leave my card and
arrange a rendezvous.   I wouldn't inter-
fere with his plans for the world ; I have
a horror of being a burden.   I'm such a
perfectly independent little body !"   She
arose and gave Beverly the fan with the
gesture of a lady fair bestowing her col-
ours upon a knight who yearned.   "Is it
far ?" she asked.

"No," answered Beverly, shortly.   "It
isn't far."

"Then let us saunter — oh, so slowly
— and drink it in."   She closed her eyes
and breathed as one overcome by the
sensuous beauty of the surroundings.

"I'm afraid I shall have to hurry,"
said the senior, with unmistakable decision.
He looked at his watch ostentatiously.
"I'm going away, and I have to pack."
She ignored the suggestion.

"Which of these mellow, world-old buildings do you live in?" she asked dreamily, stopping in the path.

"I don't live in any of them," said Beverly. He was extremely angry.

"Recluse," she murmured.

It was irritating enough, Beverly thought, to be inveigled into towing the fatuous old frump through the public streets; but the thought that his acquaintance with the lady might not end at Claverly was maddening. Billy would n't be there, of course; and it was impossible to put an unattached female cousin into his room and leave her. That particular quarter of town was not, as a rule, the most decorous on Class Day. There is always more or less, what is technically known as "trouble" in Claverly and its vicinity on Class Day afternoon. It takes the harmless form of young men with wisps of pink mosquito netting in their buttonholes, to whom the world for the time being is not such a dreary place after all; or perhaps it merely consists of innocently garbed swimming parties running foot races down the long corridors on their way to the tank. But at any rate Beverly hesitated

to turn Billy's cousin adrift there. It
would be difficult to explain his having
done so to Billy. He meant to abandon her somewhere and quickly, but not
there.

They passed out of the crowded Yard.
In his earnest desire to reach Claverly
without delay, Beverly thoughtlessly turned
into Holyoke Street. It was thronged
with carriages and summery looking girls
making for a common objective point,
half-way down on the left-hand side. He
did n't realise his mistake in having chosen
that particular route until it was too late.

"How allegro life is," remarked his
companion.

"It's very warm," answered Beverly,
increasing his pace.

"Cynic," was the reply. Beverly stared
straight ahead, but he knew the sort of expression that had accompanied the im-
putation.

"They all seem to be going in there,"
said Billy's cousin, stopping on the curbstone opposite the Pudding building.
"What is it?"

"That? Oh, somebody's spread, I suppose." Beverly went on a step or two;

but his companion did n't follow him. Just then a lady with two girls bowed to him from a victoria waiting its turn across the street.

"Are n't you coming in?" she called. Beverly went over to speak to them. The girls were exquisite creatures; he would have given his soul at that moment to be able to leave his burden on the sidewalk opposite and join them. But he was "catching a train," he explained. When he turned away, with the feeling of one about to resume a millstone, Billy's cousin was where he had left her. As he approached, she lifted a forefinger to her lips, raised her eyes mysteriously, and stood for some moments in what she probably fancied was the attitude of a listening faun.

"Music," she whispered.

"I shall certainly strangle this woman before we reach Claverly," thought Beverly.

"There is an orchestra inside," he said.

"Oh, I could just die waltzing!" she exclaimed. She crossed the street, undulating ecstatically to the music that came gaily through the open doors and windows of the Pudding.

"I really must hurry," said Beverly, very firmly.

"Just a moment," she pleaded, resting her hand on his arm and swaying ponderously from side to side in time to the waltz.

"Could anything have been more odious?" Beverly said to the fellows afterwards, when trying to explain his presence in Cambridge on Class Day. "The Pudding steps — the whole street — swarming with people on their way to the spread; a line of carriages, a block long, full of girls I knew, — *girls I knew;* and I, standing there, a ridiculous little red fan in my hand — the thing popped out, and I could n't pull it back again — with a moon-faced tub of a woman I 'd never seen before, rigged out in a crimson harness, hanging on to me as if she 'd brought me into the world, and doing some sort of a can-can on the sidewalk, like a hypnotised old cobra."

"Let 's go in," pleaded Billy's cousin, impulsively. Beverly drew away from her.

"It 's simply impossible," he said sternly. "The spread is a private one,

and I have n't even my own ticket here;
I 've lost it."

The note of irritation and despair in
his voice was overheard by a fellow in a
cap and gown who had come up behind
them just then, on his way into the
Pudding.

"That does n't make any difference,
Beverly," he said, touching his cap to the
lady; "you can come in with me all
right." Beverly turned in anguish. It
was Freddy Benson, who was helping to
give the spread. Billy's cousin became
strangely radiant; she darted a glance at
Freddy that impaled him. Beverly, she
not only impaled, but crucified.

"I have n't time to go in," said Beverly
abruptly. He was beginning to look
flushed and obstinate. Freddy opened
his eyes in polite astonishment; he was
afraid he had intruded upon a family
quarrel. The Millstone edged half way
up the Pudding steps and pouted coyly.
They stood there a moment, — Beverly,
dangerous, explosive; Freddy, mystified
and uncomfortable; the Millstone, with
her "lady fair" expression once more,
as if waiting expectantly for one of the

stalwart males to defeat the other in mortal combat and claim her for his own. People brushed by them — people Beverly knew — with glances of concern.

"You might just as well come in, you know," said Freddy, pacifically.

"You don't understand," answered Beverly, angrily.

"Just for a minute, — I promise," chimed in the Millstone; "we may find my cousin in here," she added. That possibility had n't occurred to Beverly; it was quite likely that Billy would be there at that hour. So he set his teeth and went up the steps. Freddy passed them before the big, white-gloved policeman at the door, and they pushed through the crowd in the vestibule. After a parting flutter of the eyelids at Freddy, Billy's cousin looked up at Beverly in fond disapproval.

"Naughty, naughty," she said.

The crush in the theatre of the Pudding was appalling on so warm an afternoon. But Beverly surveyed it with an exultant smile. Once separated from Billy's cousin in that jam of people, escape would be easy, pursuit impossible.

"Now follow me," he commanded, dexterously wriggling away from the arm that sought his. He meant to lead the Millstone to the corner of the room farthest away from the exit, and there, among the palms surrounding the orchestra, "wander" her like a cat in a strange wood.

"If you will be so good as to stand here," he suggested, when they had fought their way to the other end of the room, "I'll look for Fields. It may take me some time, there's such a crowd." He almost softened toward her for an instant, he was so elated at the thought of leaving her there forever in the exotic bushes, — like Ruth "in tears amid the alien corn." Then he returned her red fan, and once more became part of the crowd. He loved the crowd now as he had hated it before; it was a friendly, favouring, protecting crowd, — a crowd that rendered his movements invisible, a crowd through which large, opacous bodies in black satin could attain no velocity. Beverly made a conscientious search for Billy. He struggled around the theatre, inspected the piazza and the tent and the front rooms, and finally went upstairs to the library. But Billy was chatting, in none of the little alcove nooks, made cosey for the occasion with a prodigal display of Turkish rugs, and Beverly descended the stairs to the exit with a light heart.

The Millstone, dishevelled, apoplectic, and breathing hard, was waiting for him at the door.

"I grew faint and sought air," she explained. "Do you know what to do when a lady faints?" she went on, fanning nervously.

"Oh, yes," said Beverly, grimly; "I think I know what I should do if you fainted."

"You're giving me a very happy day," she murmured.

"It is a memorable one for me," he answered savagely.

They went out and on toward Claverly. If every man Beverly knew in college had arranged to meet him on Holyoke Street at that hour, Beverly would not have had to take off his hat many more times than he did. He bowed gravely, and had to hang on to himself to keep from calling

out as every new group of wondering
faces approached : —

"This woman does n't belong to me;
I never saw her before, and I hate her."

There were little knots of men talking on the piazzas of the clubs on
Mount Auburn Street when he turned
the corner. Out of the tail of his
eye, he could see the agitation that
seized them as he and the Millstone
came into view. Then he heard windows
opening upstairs and down, and knew,
without turning around, that from every
window craned a neck or two. He held
his breath, and prayed to Heaven that his
companion would n't take it into her head
to stop and rest, or gaze dreamily up and
down the street, or slap him with her fan.
Once safely inside Claverly, he did n't
wait to listen to her exclamations of surprise and admiration, but left her purring
to herself at the foot of the stairs and
dashed up to Billy's room. Billy was n't
there, but his door was unlatched and his
room strewn with garments. His cap
and gown were hanging over the back of
a chair. Billy was somewhere in the
building, probably in the tank, as unsus-

picious of impending catastrophe as a
playful dolphin. So Beverly hurried
down the back stairs to the tank. As he
opened the door, Billy, lying on his back
on the marble ledge, shot suddenly into
view like a long white projectile.

"I 've invented a new game," he gasped ;
"you make the marble all wet, and lie
on your back with your feet against the
wall, and then give yourself a push and —
zip ! You could go miles if there was n't
a partition. But you have to lift up
when you get to this crack, or you 'll tear
your shoulder-blades out by the roots.
Now watch me —"

"Shut up, Billy, and listen ; your cousin
is out here in the hall waiting for you."
Beverly mopped his forehead.

"My cousin ? "   Billy struggled to his
feet.

"Yes, your cousin, — a lady. Now
hurry up and get dry. I 've got to go.
She 's at the foot of the stairs. No, I 'm
not fooling, I swear to God I 'm not. It 's
the cousin you invited to Beck."

"Wait, wait, don't leave me, man.
It 'll take me hours to dress," said Billy,
piteously, dabbing himself with a bath

towel. "I have n't any cousin; I never invited one to Beck; my family is away — they 're abroad. I don't know what you 're talking about," he went on. But he continued to dry himself frantically nevertheless.

"I 'm simply telling you what I know," answered Beverly, calmly. "A person, female, aged — say forty-five; of abundant tonnage and affable manners, would like to meet blond gentleman named Fields about to graduate from Harvard; object, a family reunion. Oh, never mind your hair. Here, put on your wrapper and come on." He helped Billy, half dry, with his hair dripping stringily over his eyes, into a striped blanket covering, and pushed him gently into the hall.

The Millstone, who had been sauntering up and down the corridors in Beverly's absence, received them as they emerged.

"Oh," she said, and peered at them over the rim of her circular fan.

"Allow me to present your cousin," said Beverly, gravely.

"Cousin Marguerite," simpered the Millstone. "Can this be the little boy I used to know?" she continued, holding out her hand. "You used to wear knickerbockers." Billy drew the drapery of his striped blanket more closely about him. Shaking hands was quite out of the question. "Dear me, how you've changed."

"I'm very glad to see you," gasped Billy. "I — I wish I had my clothes on. If you'll just wait with Mr. Beverly a minute —" he turned to Beverly. "You're not in a hurry, are you?"

"Yes, I am," said the other, frankly. "I have to go to my room and then catch a train." Billy gave him the look of an offended water-spaniel.

"If I could rest somewhere until you come," suggested Cousin Marguerite.

"Couldn't you take her to your room, if you're going there anyhow?" pleaded Billy, with a tragic "I'll-do-something-for-you-some-day" expression. "If you're going there anyhow," he repeated. And once more Beverly took up his burden and set out.

He went to Beck by back streets; and he walked as fast as he possibly could, because it was hot and dusty — there were no sidewalks and no shade — and he wished to give Cousin Marguerite pain. He did n't actually want to kill her, he told himself, and marvelled, as he did so, at his own sweetness of disposition. But he hoped to succeed in disabling her in some way, by the time they reached his room, "give her a headache or break something," so that she could n't go to the Tree, or to the Beck spread, or to Memorial Hall. For he felt that other- wise she would go to them all, and he would, for some hideous reason he could n't then foresee, have to escort her. So he tore along, with Cousin Marguerite pant- ing hoarsely at his elbow, until her shoes became untied, and he had to kneel in the dust at her feet. He tied them up again — with three hard, vicious knots in each, and hurried on. Every time she placed a re- straining hand on his arm, he drew out his watch, showed it to her silently, and then remarked, " my train." He dragged her past Plympton Street, around by Bow Street, up the little hill back of Quincy, across to Beck, up the stairs two at a time and into his room, where she fell exhausted on his divan.

" Now I am going to leave you," he

announced, triumphantly. She motioned
to him feebly with her hand, and opened
her mouth as if to speak.

"You just ought to see my room at
home," she whispered, breathlessly. "It's
a perfect bower of crimson." But Beverly
did n't wait to hear about it. He ran out,
slamming the door behind him, and never
stopped nor looked behind until he
reached the club, where he called for the
longest, coldest drink the steward could
make.

"I shall never, never, see that woman
again," he said. But he did.

The club was deserted except for
Lauriston, who did n't really belong there.
Lauriston was asleep on a divan. He had
a wisp of pink mosquito netting in his
button-hole, and when Beverly roused
him, he was unable to tell where every one
had gone to so suddenly. He blinked
a moment in the light, as if he did n't even
know where he was himself, and then went
to sleep again. He was, as Beverly said,
"unfit for publication."

Just as Beverly became comfortably
settled with a gin fizz on a small table in
front of him, and a palm-leaf fan in his

hand, Billy, in cap and gown, fluttered into the club.

"Awfully good of you to take my cousin down to your room," he said, nervously. He knew with what joy Beverly must have escorted her, although he could n't very well allude to it.

"Don't mention it — charming woman —charming," murmured Beverly, politely.

"I 'm sure I don't know who she can be," went on Billy; "unless she was on the list of people my mother sent me to invite. I know I never asked her. Are you walking down that way?" he ventured, casually. Somehow or other, Cousin Marguerite seemed to him to belong as much to Beverly as to himself.

"Certainly not," answered the other, with decision. "I shall sit here until it 's time to catch the midnight train."

"And not go to the Tree or Beck or the Yard in the evening?"

"I have spoken," said Beverly, placidly.

"Well, then, good-bye." Billy held out his hand, "And don't forget you 're coming to us on the tenth." He looked troubled, and left reluctantly to find his cousin.

Beverly, true to his word, sat there fanning himself, and listening to the faint music of the band in the Yard, all the afternoon. From time to time, men dashed in to leave or get tickets, to eat something, or to find some one who never was there. They always said : —

"You here on Class Day, Beverly? I thought you were n't going to stay." Then they would rush out into the heat again to find their families and take them to the Tree. Occasionally fellows brought their fathers in to see the club and rest awhile. It amused Beverly to watch the "infants" do the honours. Prescott — six feet two — saying, "What 'll you have, Papa?" to a nice, little, old bald-headed thing, was almost as irresistible as Prescott père, when he patted his head with his handkerchief and replied, apologetically : —

"The day has been so fatiguing, and we have so much more to do later on, that I think I should like a little, a very little, rye whiskey and water."

Sears Wolcott, followed by an astonishingly young-looking gentleman who might have been Sears's older brother, if he had n't happened to be his father, was characteristic when he remarked indifferently : —

"I suppose you want something to drink ? "

Mr. Wolcott's answer struck Beverly as being equally in character : —

"Yes," he said, with a twinkle, "give me some champagne in a long glass with ice, if you think you can afford it ; I can't."

No one stayed long, and by six o'clock the club, except for Beverly and the sleeping Lauriston, was again deserted. When the steward came in to draw the curtains and turn on the lights, Lauriston awoke and asked vaguely if it was time to go to Beck.

"I suppose so," answered Beverly. "Everybody seems to have gone somewhere."

"Then I must go too," mused Lauriston, fumbling sleepily at his disordered necktie, and making a feeble attempt to smooth his hair.

"Oh, I would n't run away and leave me," suggested Beverly, "I 'm all alone." He was n't in the least anxious for Lauriston's society, but for the public good he

was willing to endure it.   Lauriston's nap
had n't proved as beneficial as it might
have ; the fellow was in no condition to
go to Beck and talk to people.

"Sorry, old man.   Can't stay.   Got to
find my mothers and sisters, and give them
'Morial tickets."   He searched his pockets,
and drew out an envelope.   Then he arose
laboriously from the divan, and, standing
before Beverly, said something that sounded
like " Delookawrite."   Beverly adjusted
his glasses : —

"No, candidly, you, don't look all
right," he declared, "and if you 're going
out to hunt for your mother and sisters, I
sincerely trust you won't find them."
Lauriston stared stupidly at the tickets in
his hand.

"Got to havvem.   Promised," he
muttered.   Beverly gently extracted the
tickets from his fingers.

"I 'll see that they get them," he said.
He had some difficulty in persuading
Lauriston that he knew Mrs. Lauriston
intimately, and would have no trouble in
finding her ; for the fellow insisted that his
mother was a most reserved woman whom
very few people knew intimately.

" She 's a reserved woman without a parasol," he said by way of identification, when he finally allowed Beverly to depart with the tickets.

The crowd on the lawn at Beck was less objectionable to Beverly, only because it was unhoused. He stopped at the top of the steps leading down to the little enclosure packed with white frocks and the startling flora and fauna of summer millinery. It was n't easy to recognise any one in the soft half light of the lanterns swinging in long festoons overhead; and it took him some time to discover Mrs. Lauriston and the girls seated around a table very near him at the foot of the steps on which he was standing. They had seen him the moment he appeared. The Millstone, sitting just behind them at the next table, with two freshmen, — distant cousins of Billy's, — also saw him.

" So you decided not to catch the train," said Mrs. Lauriston when Beverly went down to her.

" It 's harder to tear one's self away from Class Day than I thought," he said, feelingly, for he had just caught sight of Cousin Marguerite. But he

made Mrs. Lauriston a nice little bow as
he spoke.

"That's very pretty," the lady smiled
up at him; "but I should remember it
longer if we 'd seen anything of you all
day." Beverly was about to reply with the
least inane of the two inanities that came
into his mind when one of Cousin Marguerite's freshmen stood up and delivered a
message in a low tone.

"Tell her I 'm very sorry, but I can't,"
answered Beverly, changing his position
to one that defied the laws of optics to
make his eyes meet those of the Millstone. The freshman, he noticed, passed
rapidly on up the steps and out of Beck.
Beverly went on talking to Mrs. Lauriston.
He gave her the tickets, and explained
her son's failure to appear as glibly as he
could; but he was filled with horrid appre-
hensions, — Cousin Marguerite's penetrat-
ing voice rose and fell coquettishly behind
him without a pause, — and he became
noticeably ill at ease. When, in a very
few minutes, he heard the Millstone call
his own name with all the sickening lan-
guor and affectation its three syllables
could carry, he ignored the summons, and

felt himself growing rigid with anger. She called him again, a trifle louder this time — and pronounced the word " Bevaleh."

" Some one wishes to speak to you," said Mrs. Lauriston. Beverly did n't turn. " It 's the lady you were with at the Pudding; she 's sitting just behind you, and has called you twice. Don't let me keep you." Beverly turned and bowed stiffly.

" *Mauvais sujet*," said Cousin Marguerite. Mrs. Lauriston and the girls glanced at her involuntarily. Beverly left them abruptly and stood near the Millstone. If she would insist on talking to him, he preferred her playful sallies to be inaudible to the whole of Boston and its adjacent suburbs. As she turned to tap the vacant chair on her left invitingly with her red fan, the second freshman stole craftily away.

" Are you waiting for Billy ? " asked Beverly in a tone that just escaped being savage.

" I was n't waiting for Billy," she answered. Her voice was liquid with subtle meaning. " I sent him away, — dear

Billy. I'm to meet him at Memorial Hall
in a quarter of an hour. He hesitated to
leave me alone and introduced two cousins
of his — sweet boys. Then I drove him
off. And now you come; kismet, I
suppose."

"I came because you called me," said
Beverly, bluntly. "Thank you, no, I
prefer to stand; I can only stay a moment." He could n't bring himself to
the point of being deliberately rude to any
woman, — much less to a cousin of Billy's.
But he was very much annoyed at this
fatuous bore, and could n't help showing
it. His manner was decidedly icy.
Whether the Millstone realised that he
was thoroughly in earnest when he declared he could n't stay, or whether Class
Day had really been too much for her,
Beverly could n't make up his mind until
afterwards; at any rate Cousin Marguerite
suddenly let fall her fan, gave a little gasp,
and proceeded to faint. Beverly sprang
forward to prevent the rickety chair on
which she sat from upsetting, and, this
done, he looked helplessly about, as if for
suggestions. He had a hazy idea that he
ought to do something to her hands and

feet, and pour water down the front of her dress ; he had once seen that done with success. But Cousin Marguerite's feet were down in the grass under the table somewhere ; her hands too seemed rather inaccessible, — she had fallen forward and hidden them. If he should leave her to go for a glass of water, she would undoubtedly slide off her chair and get walked on. In his distress, Beverly called to Mrs. Lauriston. Mrs. Lauriston brought some apollinaris from her table, held it to the Millstone's lips, and dabbed it on her temples with a handkerchief.

" Ought n't I — ought n't you to ' loosen something ' ? " asked Beverly, giving the crimson necktie a wrench. Cousin Marguerite's eyelids fluttered with returning life. All she needed was air, she said, looking about her in bewilderment.

" If Mr. Beverly will kindly take me to the street — to the open — How very stupid of me ; I have n't done it since I was a girl," she added. So Beverly thanked Mrs. Lauriston hastily, and left the Beck spread with Cousin Marguerite on his arm. Outside she leaned against the great red letter-box on the corner, gasped a

little, arranged her necktie and dried her
temples. Then she passed her arm through
Beverly's again and started for Memorial
— to find Billy. Consciousness had returned, but it had not brought to the Millstone strength enough to enable her to
walk alone. There was simply no pretext on which Beverly could leave Billy's
cousin now. For although he was convinced that her indisposition was what he
called " a cheap bluff at dying," he could n't
very well act on that assumption. He
accepted the fact that he would have to
stay by her, maddening as she was, until
they found Billy.

She was maddening. She insisted on
going to Memorial by way of the Yard,
and loitered shamelessly on the way —
she said she felt strangely faint — to
enjoy the crowd, the music, and the
glow of the lanterns among the elms.
She watched the dancing at Memorial
until Beverly wondered audibly why Billy
did n't come ; at which she announced
blandly : —

" He said he would meet me at the
steps — right near the mandolins and
banjos. I have n't seen any, have you ? "

The mandolins and banjos were, of course, on the steps of the Law School, as Cousin Marguerite very well knew.

"I wish you had told me that sooner," said Beverly, controlling himself. "Billy has probably tired of waiting and gone away."

"Oh, well —" she sighed. Ever since the two had left Beck, the Millstone had hovered shrewdly between apoplexy and intense enjoyment of everything she saw; she relied on the one to disarm criticism of the other. Billy was n't in front of the Law School; but his cousin thought it best to wait a few minutes longer for him, besides, the Mandolin Club was just about to play. She closed her eyes when the music began — the piece was a Spanish something or other through which a tambourine shivered at intervals — and clung to Beverly's arm.

"The Italians are so passionate," she murmured at the end.

"Billy is n't coming," said Beverly.

"I 'm afraid we 've missed him," she assented.

"And the evening is almost over; you 've seen everything," Beverly went

on.   "It *is* over," he added joyously ; a
drop of rain had fallen on his hand.

"Class Day is dead; the angels weep,"
mused Cousin Marguerite, sentimentally.
" ' I warmed both hands before the fire of
life.   It sinks — ' "

"And are you 'ready to depart'? " asked
Beverly, eagerly ; Cousin Marguerite had
shied at the really vital clause of the
quotation.

" 'Come, chaos — I have seen the
best,' " was her answer.

But Beverly did n't consider that he
had seen the best, until the bridge car that
was to bear away Cousin Marguerite appeared in Harvard Square.   He would
have rushed off — the rain had begun in
earnest — as soon as his companion of the
afternoon and evening was seated, had she
not extended her plump hand for a last,
lingering pressure.

"Good-bye," she said, softly. "There
are some things one cannot express;
they are here," she touched her chest
lightly with the finger-tips of her left hand.
"Good-bye. Oh, — I forgot to tell you,"
she added abruptly, in another tone; " Billy
and I discovered that we don't spell our

names the same way.   We spell ours with an 'e.'   We found it out just after he had refreshed me at Beck Hall and introduced those two sweet boys.   So you see, Billy is more than a cousin; he is a friend."

The Millstone's good-bye smile was an inscrutable performance, in which Beverly thought he detected pity, amusement, and a sort of devilish self-satisfaction.   He turned, without a word, to find Billy.

THE END

THIS BOOK IS PRINTED BY JOHN WILSON
AND SON CAMBRIDGE MASSACHUSETTS
DURING DECEMBER 1897